Fiona Cooper was born in Bristol in 1955, moved to London in 1973 and now lives on Tyneside. She has been writing ever since she can remember: her short stories have appeared in *Cosmopolitan*, *Passion Fruit* (Pandora Press) and *Woman's Day* in Australia and she is the author of three other novels: *Rotary Spokes*, *Heartbreak on the High Sierra* (also published by Virago) and *Jay Loves Lucy*. *Not the Swiss Family Robinson*, Fiona Cooper's latest novel, shows that her fast-paced and witty fiction goes from strength to strength.

NOT THE SWISS FAMILY ROBINSON

Fiona Cooper

VIRAGO

Published by Virago Press Limited 1991
20–23 Mandela Street, Camden Town, London NW1 0HQ

*A CIP catalogue record for this book is available from
the British Library.*

Typeset by CentraCet, Cambridge
Printed in Great Britain by
Cox & Wyman Ltd, Reading, Berkshire

With thanks to Alison, Caroline, Sue,
Jenny, Dee, Monika, Jenny, Susan, Alison,
Julia and Maureen.

1

I read *The Swiss Family Robinson* when I was nine, and I say shit. The teacher must have thought she was real smart giving it to me, seeing I was Monica Robinson and my family was as near to the middle of nowhere as you can get without adventures and shipwrecks. The nearest town was What Cheer, twenty miles away, a few dozen streets of houses, a school, a garage, a general store/cafe/bar combination and workshops to make do and mend any kind of farm implement or machinery. The land was rough, tough and dry, hard on even the best equipment, and Pop never could see the sense of buying new.

'A man gotta be cautious, Kathereen,' he growled at my mother. We had a yard full of rusting junk to testify to Pop's caution.

The Swiss Family Robinson just stumbled across everything they needed, from an agouti to a zebra-skin rug, by way of a wrecked ship stocked better than a Sears catalogue not more than a paddle away from an island paradise. All this and fields of wild potatoes, calabashes, medicinal figs and coconut milk that turned to wine in an hour or so. Swiss Family Robinson – yo!

Old Pastor Robinson left my Pop standing. That boy could have built a split-level ranch house in three weeks out of matchsticks and planted an apple orchard by way of amusement in his lunch hour. My Pop could never find one piece of timber when it was needed, though there was a yard in town. Our house looked like it had seen better times and was doing very nicely without any fancy patching, thank you. And where the good Pastor was a mine of information on any flora or fauna his golden-haired, rosy-cheeked offspring chose to drag home, my Pop had trouble enough dragging crops out of our red earth to get by. And me and Rosemarie and Scoot my brother had more

1

sense than to ask him anything. What the hell I send you to school for, said Pop.

The sky was wide and generally blue, and I knew we were different only when I went to school and all the other kids had pencils with their names on and got picked up in shiny cars where we used anything doled out of the teacher's desk, and hung around late for the dirt-red bus, groaning its slow way to all the farms scattered around What Cheer. But Mom said to pay no mind to folk with more money than sense, and she knew everything worth knowing.

One day the schoolteacher drove all the way to our house with a cotton bag full of other children's clothes.

'I thought you might be able to do something with them, Mrs Robinson,' she said, in an angel of mercy voice.

Mom picked out one shirt like it was a floor rag.

'I never did figure on mending stuff for other folks' kids,' she said.

'Oh no, Mrs Robinson, they're for your children. I know times are hard.'

'Times are what they always been,' said Mom like the Queen of Sheba.

I was proud of her. I knew that shirt. It came off the hide of a kid I was always having to punch out. Jason Morgan Sole, for Christ's sake. I was not about to put things on my back he had no use for.

'Looks like a wasted trip, Miss Er,' said Mom, 'Can I offer you some refreshment?'

'Well, if it's no trouble.'

'The day hospitality is trouble my name ain't Robinson.'

The teacher sat on the porch, on a chair she'd dusted off first and drew her skirts round her like she might catch something. Mom went into the kitchen and I heard her muttering about high-falutin noses stuck into other folks' business. In ten minutes flat the table was full of plates and dishes, piled high with biscuits, bread, cheese, preserves and even a ham.

'Ha!' she said to the table, then fluted out to the porch, 'Would you care to step in, Miss Er, and have a bite. Just a something like I fix for the kids every day after school.'

My brother Scoot's eyes were wide as a harvest moon, but you could count on him saying nothing, being as his mouth was stuffed full from start to finish. I thought I'd back Mom up a little.

'Hey, Mom,' I said, 'I don't know as I can eat much, not after the hog we slaughtered this morning and ate at lunchtime.'

Eat your heart out, Pastor Robinson, with your little wife and pretty, handsome, spirited, bold, thoughtless, intelligent, well-informed Franz, Fritz, Jack and Ernest! Mom gave me a deal-with-you-later smile.

'Eat.'

Then Pop elected to come in from wherever he'd been sleeping it off. Pop was never sober, but never so drunk you'd notice if you didn't know him.

'Company,' he said carefully. 'Well, how do, Miss?'

'Willard,' said Mom. 'Git washed and come and eat.'

Pop got. He was more like a shadow round the place than anything much else. Once in a long while he'd start roaring at Mom and me and Rosemarie would plan how we'd kill him. But when I told this to Mom she said to pay him no mind, and he'd never been the same since he quit the Air Force in the late fifties.

So when the teacher left, she carried away her raggetty-taggetty charity bag, a jar of pickles, a fruit loaf and an invitation she never took up to call by any time she was passing.

'Now, miss,' said Mom, with a lot of steel and half a twinkle, 'A lie is a lie. And you don't tell 'em. But it was a good lie. Everybody knows you don't raise hogs on this land. But that teacher, she knows nothing outside of school-talk and charity. Nothing.'

'Tell me a story, Mom,' I said at bedtime, trading on her battle-won good mood. It was always worth asking. Mom's stories weren't the kind you read in children's books. They were all true and no endings, happy or otherwise.

'I'll be glad to sit for a moment. You ever hear about the time Scoot was born?'

'No.' Another lie.

'Well now. If I live to be a hundred and foolish, I'll never see storms like the week Scoot was coming. Sky all black and purple, and four solid days when we never saw the sun. Winds that ripped out the tree roots and tossed the trees around like they were tumbleweeds. And then the rain came. Did I say rain? It was like an ocean had been lifted up and dumped straight down on us all at one time. And then I knew Scoot was coming. When your Pop got out the wagon, the wheels got swallowed right down into the mud. We'd have needed a rowboat to get to town. That enough for you, miss?'

That's how it always was with Mom's stories. Did I ever tell you about the heat snap we had? We were eating dust sandwiches, drinking cups full of dust, and for six months after I was washing red dust out of every garment. That enough for you? Or the time Rosemarie was born. That was in Germany, and Pop had a uniform that made him look like an admiral, not just an airman. There was a blizzard on the way to the hospital so they had to leave the car, and the snow was so thick it turned them into walking snowmen. At the hospital not a living soul spoke English, and there were people turned bright blue with cold dying in the corridors. That enough for you?

'Tell me about when I was born, Mom.'

'That's enough. I got work to do.'

She never did tell me how it was when I was born and after a while I stopped asking and worked it out for myself. If Scoot had arrived on a torrent like Moses, and Rosemarie was born like Jesus in snowy Bethlehem, then I must have come in on the tail of a twister and landed on the roof. Hurricane Monica.

None of us did too good at school after the Visitation, and Scoot was always fighting. I recall the Lady Gracious teacher talking to me after school once.

'Monica, does Scoot get into trouble at home?'

'No, ma'am.'

I heard her talking about 'loyalty' with the other teacher and I knew she'd mistook me. I never saw Scoot outside mealtimes. None of us did. He spent all his time in the barn loft where he'd put up a sign: DEADLY PRIVATE. We never bothered to snoop. Trouble? None of us ever did anything much to get into trouble. My rules were not to worry Mom, and to steer clear of Pop when he was talking drunk. The idea seemed to be that we would work on the farm when we left school. It had always been that way, ours had always been bad land, we got by and I couldn't imagine anything different.

There were highlights in the year: the Easter Carnival at What Cheer, when we combed the ground for dimes, sneaked through the tent flaps, made ourselves sick with candyfloss and the roller-coaster ride. All the bums in What Cheer scraped themselves up off the sidewalk for the week of the Carnival, and hung around while the rides were setting up, twitching for the magic words:

'You want a job?'

They got a little beer money taking tickets, fixing the safety bars across or just running around looking busy. One of the bums was known as the Octopus, seeing as that's where he always worked. The rest of the year he said nothing and did even less, but at the Carnival he swanked like a king. You paid the cashier in her glass box, stumbled along the boardwalk, and the Octopus strutted you to a carriage with *Zap!* or *Pow!* or *Zowie!* screaming in scarlet and gold paint a foot high across the back. He clanged the bar across, fumbled the catch shut and spun you round. Then the ride jerked on one, and the carriage lurched into the air. Gradually the ground fell away, and you could see down on to people's heads and smell the diesel smoking out of the throbbing generators, smell the burning sugar and the hamburgers and hot dogs and onions. It was a fairyland down there, with strings of bright lights on every stall, flashing rainbow galaxies of bulbs strewn along every whirling girder.

With every lurch the sounds changed, and Tamla Motown belted over the sizzling bumper-car ride *Do you really love me, baby?* The Bluegrass Boys swore *for ever to be tree-ew! To the one and only yeee-ew!!* while couples bumped and swayed along the Cakewalk. Finally the Octopus would stand back to check every carriage was full. His red stubbled face would split into a grin and:

'Hold tight for a fast ride, *folks!*' he bellowed, and waved one filthy hand at the cashier like he owned the whole show. She would land a needle on a crackling disc, and yank the metal rod to start us whirling in earsplitting rock 'n' roll. And as we dipped and screamed, every so often we'd sweep by scarlet cheeks and a beer bottle upended in the middle of the Octopus's happy face.

On the way home Mom would say we'd nearly given her a coronary, and let the Octopus be a lesson to us about drinking. Pop would laugh at this and say:

'There but for the grace of God and the love of a good woman, Kathereen!'

We'd fall asleep to them bickering. That was the only talking they did.

Every year someone would write to the *What Cheer Argus*, complaining about standards, unseemly behaviour and Sodom and Gomorrah, and the next year it would all be forgotten, as the baroque pageant of the Carnival tottered upright once more in all its gaudy finery, planted on old beer crates, breeze-blocks and ancient timbers.

And there was the Annual Farm Show, when we all went to look at the biggest ears of wheat and the meatiest steers. Pop never had anything to exhibit in this line and spent the days in the beer tent. I went to find him one year, and there he was squaring up to a big man, feet sliding everywhere, fists wild, slurring out insults. The man was just punching him away and shouting stuff like:

'Willard Robinson, you couldn't teach a settin' hen to cluck!'

I wanted Pop to knock him to the ground, but he was the first to fall and lay there roaring. The man spotted me, and picked me up.

'Come on, princess, you can't help your daddy being who he is.'

He bought me a soda, and I poured it on the ground. He only laughed and said I'd a thing or two to teach my daddy, yessir! I hated him.

The best bit for me was the tinsel and red-dust rodeo ring. The first time I saw it, me and Mom had worked through the crowd, elbows banging my head, and my hand locked in hers. Suddenly we were right by the railings, with the music blaring through my head, loud as the midday sun. The rodeo riders paraded round with spurs of gleaming silver and glossy boots in every colour. They were gods, towering above me through the rose-coloured dust. They had fancy shirts embroidered and rhinestoned all over, and a loose, lazy way of sitting smiling and waving their hats at us all. The dust settled and then it all took off, the splintering smash as the barrier flung open, and the god catapulted out on a mad-eyed bucking sweating horse, tossed up and over, hanging on to a wild hank of mane. And then a crash to the dirt fit to break every bone in their body. But

6

they'd pick themselves up, grab their hats, and slap the dust from their pants. They walked out of that ring with an idle swagger like they were going no place special, but they knew damn well every eye was watching them go there. I lost Mom's hand, and I didn't care one bit. I wanted to be a rodeo rider when I grew up, but I could never get our good old horses to do more than a gentle canter for all I'd whoop and hey at them. And there was no way I'd use spurs.

When I was about twelve, my sister started walking out with a boy called Billy Bob Welch. He had a pick-up truck and off they would ride.

'Back by ten y'hear,' Mom said, all proud and damned if she'd show it.

I heard sisters are supposed to confide in each other, but I never knew a thing about Billy Bob and what they did. I never much liked him. He was the kind that says, 'hey, little sis', and punches your arm. Besides, Rosemarie went all giggly and high-voiced when he was around.

Then her and Billy Bob were fixing to get married. This worried me. I couldn't see her happy with him. He seemed set on drinking and bragging, which is OK for seventeen but from what I could see, he'd just be Pop all over again in twenty years' time. The most my sister said was that at least this way she'd get away from home, and she advised me to do myself up pretty soon and get to a dance to find a beau, cuz there was no other way for a girl to leave her home. Me, I figured anything Huck Finn could do I could, and the Mississippi was not the only river. Besides, soon as I got me a rodeo horse I'd be off for glory into the sunset.

As for walking out with a boy, I couldn't see it. Since I'd left the first school, I'd had a crush on Joanne Lee Hunter, four years and a world away from me. I only had to see her for my heart to start thumping and my breath to speed up like I'd been running. I had dreams of riding the rodeo and getting the trophy and giving it to her so she'd know just how I felt. As for dancing, I knew it wasn't for me, and I had a sense folk would think it strange for two girls to dance together. When I closed my eyes to think about it, it was always Joanne I saw, spinning round the floor in my arms. I hadn't even spoken to her, there just wasn't the opportunity, but I knew she was The One. I

7

began to wonder if I should have been born a boy, it would have made everything a little plainer for me. Kissing and all that stuff. Finally I decided the only thing was dreaming. I was not going to have a love-life beyond dreaming things I knew were so bad and impossible there wasn't a word to describe them.

Then we had a real English teacher from England, Miss Margaret Courtland. She even got the worst in the class eating out of her hand. Whether it was her voice, like something out of an old-fashioned movie, or what, we all sat silent and lapped up every word. She was teaching about Courtly Love, and it all fell into place for me. I knew about honour, what with the chase-me-devil thoughts I was having about Joanne Lee Hunter. Courtesy. Chivalry. *Though I am nothing to her/Though she may rarely look at me/I'll love her till I die*. Yeah.

Never to even talk to the Beloved, but worship her at a distance. I lived what those knights felt. Only to see her! Only to hear her name! I had been hanging around at recess wherever I could see Joanne for two years. Miss Margaret Courtland was the first teacher ever to give me As.

The week before Billy Bob and my sister got married, we heard in assembly that Joanne Lee Hunter was leaving the state and going East. It might as well have been Mars. Everybody liked her: she was real hot at all games, a model student, and prettier than I'd ever seen or hoped for. When the Principal said how we all would miss her, I thought I would pass out on the floor. What did the day hold beyond a hope of seeing her? I felt the years without her stretch ahead of me like so many miles on a desert road. I planned to stow away in her parents' car, I dreamed of hitching miles to land on her doorstep, I pictured her alone and friendless and me being there and making it all better. I wrote a dozen letters begging her to run away with me. And trashed them all. The days raced by to the countdown of my heart.

Her last day at school I was numb head to foot. At home they were busy doing the house out for the wedding. I felt like I'd wear black for the rest of my life. It was the worst day. I had to talk to her.

I hung around the crowd of autographing, photographing

students. Finally I was in front of her, so close I could see her beautiful mouth, all smiles.

'Well, who are you?' she said.

'It's Rosemarie's sister,' said someone.

'Oh! You must be excited!' said Joanne, 'Isn't she marrying Billy Bob Welch tomorrow?'

I love you, don't go, I can't bear it . . .

'Yeah,' I said.

'Well, you give her my love, you hear? And pass this on!'

And then she kissed me on the cheek.

I stumbled away. She kissed me! But it was for my sister and for Billy Bob. I had blown the only chance I'd have to tell her. It was the end of my life.

I hardly slept through that longest night, and in the morning the wedding went on around me like a nightmare. Mom had gone wedding crazy and made me a snow-white dress all over ribbons and bows. I started slugging away at the punch I'd seen Pop concocting and tasting all the evening before. Hadn't I heard him say liquor takes away your troubles? It made me pleasantly numb and I figured I'd better find a place to sit quiet for a while, when the floor started looping the loop under my feet. I was sitting near my Pop who was delighted at the excuse of a wedding to tie on a real load, enough not to notice who was by him. He was drinking with Billy Bob's Pop, Harry Welch, the man who'd made such a fool of him in the Farm Show beer tent. Neither one of them seemed to remember it. Jesus! They were real buddies now, and Pop was matching Harry from his own bottle. They'd done away with the pretence of glasses.

'Willard,' said Billy Bob's Pop, 'I am mightily pleased at this here wedding. You got a fine girl there.'

'A fine girl,' said Pop in a thick echo.

'Soon have to be thinkin' about a young man for Monica, Willard.'

'Harry, she don't appear to show no interest,' said Pop confidingly.

'She's always been strong-willed, Willard, a real little spitfire, but I guess she'll be getting a good little figure on her soon, if she's anything like your Rosemarie. Pretty girls seem to run in your family!'

9

'I can't see it with Monica,' said Pop, nodding foolishly.

'Willard, your Rosemarie is the spit of Katherine, and you know I'd have married her if you hadn't got there first, yuh lucky dawg.'

Then there was a lot of hitting each other on the back, yessiring and belly laughs like belching.

'Have you noticed, Harry, c'm here, have you noticed anything about Monica?'

Billy Bob's Pop leaned close.

'She don't favour neither one of us, Harry,' slurred Pop. 'And there is a reason for this.'

'Whuh?' said Harry.

By now they were leaning so close one of them was sure to fall into the other's lap. Pop put a finger to his lips and shushed.

'C'm here. I'm telling you, Harry, Monica ain't ours.'

'Whuh?'

'No, sir. We had Rosemarie in Germany. When I was in th'Air Force, best time of my life, boy, best time. And then Kathereen was set on having another. And the doctor said she warn't likely to do that. We went to England after that, and, listen to me, Harry, we adopted Monica. Yessir, we took her in and gave her a home and I gave her my name. There wasn't no need to tell folks when we come back, specially since we had the boy since. The doctor got it wrong, huh. Nothing wrong in that department, boy! What the hell, a big happy family we always been, Harry. Two girls and a boy. But Monica ain't ours.'

They leaned back and took a little refreshment.

'Damned if you ain't a Christian couple,' said Billy Bob's Pop.

'I'll drink to that,' said Pop, and they started talking about horses and feed and grandchildren.

2

'Monica, are you all right, child?'

It was Mom. I'd been sitting kind of paralysed with a mish-mash of thoughts spinning wildly around me, trying to put words to my questions, and here was Mom, fussing over me. Mom?

'I been sampling the punch,' I told her through the haze.

'Goddamighty, child, what am I to do with you? You didn't get that drinking from my family!'

But she was laughing and then she was busy again, seeing to her guests. After a while Pop was roaring about clearing up the big room so we all could do some dancing. I saw him and his boozing buddy, Harry, nudging each other and looking over at me, like I was a prize cow or a pet poodle. Oh, so I was going to dance, was I, with whatever young man they thrust my way for a partner? I stared at Pop, fumbling at the table edge and lurching backwards and forwards trying to straighten it against the wall, his wet red mouth jabbering and laughing.

Given me his name, had he, like I was a dog he'd rescued?

I escaped into the cool night. Let them dance and sing and sway around like fools – I wanted no part of it. Ahead of me the plain stretched for ever, under a translucent bell of navy sky, with its ice-white stars. I walked away from the house. I could breathe cleaner out here, and didn't look back till I got to the yard gate.

My, what fun they did appear to be having in the house! Mad shadows jogged around on the blinds, demon heads horned with party hats, distorted mouths gurgling from lumpy great tankards, and the clanging and twanging and yipping and bouncing of Tennessee Tex and his Outplain Boys, who were only there cuz Tennessee Tex was a cousin of Billy Bob's Pop and didn't require a fee for 'family'. Oh, they'd talk about this

11

night for months to come and what a good time they all had had. *We gave her a good wedding, din' we, gave 'em a good start out, din' we, Kathereen?* I could hear Pop praising himself up to the skies and back again for the next few years, every time he made a buck or two.

The cold air had finally reached my brain. What the hell was I to do next? The dirt road to What Cheer glittered in the moonlight: I could be in town and through the other side by dawn if I started walking now. Yeah! *Yeah?* In your cutesy-pie virgin-white organza and patent dancing shoes – forget it! I'd have to sneak back in and change. I didn't have a cent to my name and was not fool enough to imagine I'd get far. Our state line was over a hundred miles away in any direction.

The front door slammed. I flattened myself down like a tree stump and took a sideways look. A dark figure slouched along the side of the house. It was only Scoot. I waited till his shadow had melted into the solid black of the barn, and flitted across the yard and round the back of the house.

'*Ef yew really lerve me, Be honest with me . . .*' wailed Tennessee Tex through the floorboards, to the sound of a fiddle, glasses clinking and heavy feet shuffling out of time. In minutes I was back in my jeans and a shirt, and hauled my jacket on. Goodbye to my room and this house of strangers! I looked in the moonlit mirror. Shit! My hair was all curls and a white ribbon – I was Calamity Jane and Shirley Temple all in one. Thank you, Mom! I tore the ribbon out, wet my hair and yanked a comb through to flatten it out. It was time to go. I froze on the landing as the music blared louder. Someone had opened the hall door.

'Whar's my baby girl?' Pop was hollering at the foot of the stairs.

'Hush up, Willard. Leave her be. It's you and your drinking ways sent her outta here,' I heard Mom hiss at him, then there was a stumbling crash. The music was muffled again as the door slammed shut. I tiptoed downstairs. Pop was a snoring heap flat on the floor, one hand gripped round an upright bottle. Even in his sleep, he never spilt a drop.

But . . . he was so far gone I went and stood right over him. His belly was a taut dome under checkered cotton. One pocket was stiff and square on the mound – I slid out the wad of bills, 'weddin' expenses, Kathereen!' He owed me. I backed away through the kitchen and out on to the back porch.

So now, go now? Travel by night and sleep by day?

I stood shivering in a shadow and looked around. For the last time. The sagging line of the roof against the sky. The pot-holed waste of the yard. The gate twisting off its one good hinge. The patched barn. The spindly web of rusting metal that had been a harvester and such a real bargain Pop had almost done a half-acre with it before it seized up.

And beyond it all, the world.

I had to talk to someone before I left. Mom was all tied up with *company*, Rosemarie I'd left clutching Billy Bob's foolish arm. I went over to the barn, ears ringing with cold. Inside I could smell the tattered bales of straw solid with dust.

'Hey, Scoot, can I come up?'

There was a scuffling like a hundred rats above me, and Scoot's head appeared silhouetted in candlelight against the square trapdoor.

'Who the hell is that?'

'It's me, Monica.'

'Pop send you over to get me?'

'Hell no, Scoot, he's passed out in the hall.'

'Mom send you over?'

'She don't even know you're gone nor me neither. I just wanted to talk to someone.'

Scoot slid a ladder down towards me in the blackness. I climbed up. As soon as I was in the loft, he hauled the ladder back up, and slid the trapdoor over again.

'You better sit down,' he said, putting the candle on an orange-crate.

I hadn't been in the loft since I was a kid, before Scoot took it over. He'd made it real comfortable, with packing-case cupboards, and straw swathed in old curtain material for seats. He'd tacked pictures up all over the sloping roof, come-hither blonde women, and a hundred and one views of Mack trucks.

'Well goddam, you're my first visitor. You want a drink? What'll you have? I got most everything up here,' he said with a swagger, opening up a crate full of bottles.

'What're you drinking?'

'Most of the time I drink beer. I got Collins mix too. And a little bourbon. I put the Collins in the beer sometimes. It's real good. I call it the Scoot Deluxe.'

'OK.'

I recognised our school water glasses and raised mine to my brother. Half-brother. No kind of brother at all. The boy who'd been raised beside me.

'They still going for it down there?'

'Yeah. They cleared the room for dancing now.'

'Sheeee–it!' said Scoot, and offered me a cigarette.

'I never knew you smoked, Scoot. Thanks.'

'I been smoking since I was eleven,' he said, and flicked a fancy lighter my way. Smart boy – the school had been torn apart searching for this same lighter six months before: a college presentation to the Principal.

This small gift has sentimental value, and I appeal to all students for its return.

But the Principal never had appealed to Scoot Robinson.

'What really pisses me,' said Scoot, blowing fastidious rings, 'is when he starts doing that graveyard shuffle with any woman too polite to tell him to go screw. And Mom just stands there and takes it, kind of smiling like she had something to apologise for.'

No need to ask who 'he' was.

I gulped the Scoot Deluxe.

'Yeahrr!' said Scoot deliberately, flicking ash with a twist of his bony wrist, 'You recall when Daisy Ann Mayhew got hitched to that appliance salesman? I coulda smacked Pop into the ground, dribbling down Daisy Ann's Mom's neck. And Mom all bright and breezy and making the best of it, saying, *ain't he having a good time, Scoot, baby, maybe you'll be a dancer when you're grown, your Pop always knew how to move his feet.* Piss on him!'

He heaved himself on to one elbow and waved his cigarette at me.

'I guess you're all hunky-dory with them over at the house, huh, Monica? You and Rosemarie?'

'Jesus, Scoot. I haven't had what you'd call a conversation with Rosemarie since Billy Bob first drove his truck into this yard. What do you reckon to Billy Bob?'

Scoot flopped down on his back.

'I don't reckon shit to shit,' he said. 'Gimme your glass. You wanna hear some real music?'

'Sure.'

So that's where the Band of Hope cassette player disappeared

to! Scott measured me another drink and rattled through a box
of cassettes.

'Yeah,' he said, switching it on. 'This is Raver Ridley and the
Nightliners. Truckin' music.'

> *'Whoa! I'm lookin' at the world through a windshield*
> *And I see ever'thin' in a little bit different light*
> *Got a sweet little thing I'm wantin' t' see in Nashville*
> *Goin' down round Dallas and rollin' on South tonight.'*

'That's it,' said Scoot with satisfaction. 'This here America's
so wide and high a man could drive for ever and never go the
same way twice. Gonna get myself a rig and blow.'

'You gonna do that?' I'd never heard Scoot say as much as a
sentence before.

'Yup. Get myself a licence when I'm sixteen, work my ass off
till twenty, fix me up a bulldog rig, and you won't see no more
Scoot round here. Course I might drive offa the highway once
in a while, pull up outside the yard and see Mom. I can't wait
till I get my growth, Monica. Pop won't dare open his mouth to
me.'

'Thought you were going to take over the farm?'

'No point arguing with Pop and his whisky dreams. This
farm ain't never going to make it – JESUS CHRIST! How he can
blabber on. Next year we gonna plant sweet peas, Kathereen!
Next year's gonna be a good year for mustard seed! Yessir, next
year. Next year the Good Fairy's gonna come down and wave
her itty-bitty wand, and it's gonna be Christmas every day!'

'Oh, the white line is the lifeline of the nation!' growled Raver
Ridley.

'Yo!' said Scoot.

The barn door shuddered open below us.

'Shit!' whispered Scoot, his face going into a hunted mask.

'Hey, boy! It's your Poppa! Scoot, goddammit, where are you?'

Scoot flipped off the hay-bale and slithered across the floor to
lift the trapdoor.

'What you want, Pop?'

'Damn it boy! You got a girl up there, hi hi, huh?'

'What if I do?' Scoot's voice echoed Pop's leer.

'Damned if you ain't my boy! You seen Monica?'

'Waall, I don't like to say nothin', Pop. I seen her sliding down across the yard a while back.'

'Aw, Jesus, your Mom's creatin' in the house. Which way was she headed?'

'Waaall, Pop,' said Scoot, all man-of-the-world, 'She wasn't lackin' for company.'

'No!' Pop slapped his thigh.

'Yeah,' said Scoot, 'I'd leave her be, Pop.'

'Right, boy,' said Pop, like he'd found a million-buck lottery ticket, 'Yee–ha, boy! Don't let me disturb you and your lady friend no more. Goddamn! Monica have got herself a beau!'

'Sorry about that shit, Monica,' said Scoot, 'but it's the only way to get the lousy drunk outta your hair.'

'Yeah. He seems set on getting me my very own Billy Bob.'

'You got a boyfriend?' Scoot asked carefully.

'No. No offence, Scoot, but I don't want one. You got a girlfriend?'

'I got a few in mind,' said Scoot, grinding out his cigarette, 'but no one serious. Jesus, everyone in this county wants a wedding ring the minute they lose their teething ring. No, I got something else in mind. Look above you. There's my girls.'

I looked up at Patsy Cline, Dolly Parton and Bette Midler. The boy had taste.

'Here's to your girls, Scoot,' I said, and downed the last of my drink.

'How's about you, Monica? Clint Eastwood? Robert Redford? Clark Gable? I lie here some nights thinking about it. I can have anyone I want, lying here. Come to Poppa, baby! When I get my rig I can have a girl in every town till I meet the right one!'

We smoked on in silence for a while. Scoot jack-knifed upright all of a sudden and changed the music.

'God!' he said reverently, 'I can turn into Superman listening to Dakota Staton.'

The velvet voice, the thrilling violins, the shudder of guitar . . . all these things, the Scoot Deluxe, the farce of the wedding, the empty days without Joanne Lee Hunter – all this and being adopted too. I rolled over and snuffled into my coat-sleeve.

'Hey, I can change the music, Monica. Shit,' said Scoot, patting at my shoulder anxiously.

16

'Don't you fuckin dare,' I said through my fist, 'I just want to go with it.'

'Yo, sis,' he said softly, and I heard the soft sloosh of liquor near my ear.

'Can you keep your mouth shut, Scoot? I'm asking you. I have to say some things out loud and I don't want any answers. And I don't want anyone to know, but damn, if you can't keep your mouth shut, I'll go and shout it out to the goddam fields, boy!'

'You notice me blabbing all over town? Spill it, Monica.'

I sat up, and took another gulp at the Deluxe.

'My life fell apart yesterday and today. You ask me about a boyfriend. Shit! I've been in love for three years now, and I just learned the one I love is going so far away I'll never see – them – again. Then I'm listening to *him* bullshitting on to Billy Bob's Pop, the pair of them so plastered they make City Hall look like naked brick. And *He* just lets drop, just lets slip, by way of drinkin talk, like you might be talking about the goddam weather or what goddam crop to plant, *He* just chooses to tell a total stranger that I'm fuckin adopted, me, Monica Robinson, I'm not Monica Robinson, I've been picked out of a row of baby cots like a fuckin lottery prize, and *He* has the fuckin *GALL* to sit there patting himself on his fuckin *HOGback* for being so *CHRISTIAN* and *GENEROUS* as to give me his *NAME*, for Chrissake!'

'*My funny Valentine, sweet tender Valentine . . .*' poured out of the cracked speakers like cream. I saw two red dots in the gloom. Scoot handed me a cigarette.

'So I went out in the yard, Scoot, all ready to leave home, and there I am in a party dress, all ribbons and curls, and not a cent to my name. So I put my clothes on, took a wad outta Pop's pocket, and then I saw the barn. Shit is, I don't know where to go. That's what brought me up here. To my baby brother who isn't even my brother. Although so fuckin what? Just sign a piece of paper and give a girl a good home and family. And whatever you do, don't tell her about it! I mean, it's only my fuckin life, Scoot.'

'Can I talk?' said Scoot, very quietly.

'Go ahead, bro, I'm through talking.'

'If you want to get away, Monica, and I guess you do, don't

do it tonight. *OK?* Things have to be planned. You could get to college. Jesus, I've had my brainy sister shoved down my neck for years. *Why can't you apply yourself like Monica, Scoot?* Nearest college is 300 miles north of here. It's a step. Or at least get yourself a weekend job, and start stashing them bills, woman. You can't get out without money to get you going. So you rolled Pop tonight: stash it. When he's drunk unconscious you can get the odd five spot to help it along. And you ought to talk to the pair of them. Him and Mom. They ought to tell you more about this adoption – you ain't putting me on, Monica?'

'Sure as shit stinks.' I spat.

'Pheeeee–ow!' said Scoot. 'What did he say about that, aside from him being a true-blue red-hot Holy Poppa?'

'Oh, something about the doctor said Mom couldn't have no more kids, but they still wanted some, so they got me, and then you came along anyway. So they didn't even need to have me.'

'You got a consolation prize anyhow,' said Scoot. 'Can you imagine how *good* I feel knowing I got Robinson blood flowing through my veins? Mom I can take, but the idea of *him* and his fucked-up genes making me! I almost decided to take the pledge on account of him. But I guess I can handle it better than him. Here's hoping!'

Scoot raised his glass, and stuck a new candle over the guttering end of the old one. I could hear him breathing in the darkness while he lit the wick. He slotted another cassette in. One I hadn't heard before.

'Who's this?'

'John Lennon. Listen to him! *Beautiful, beautiful, beautiful boy!* That's his son. Jesus! *Life is what happens when you're busy making other plans!* Fuckin poetry! Can you imagine having a daddy who writes you songs? Pop has trouble writing his own name. What kind of daddy do you think yours was?'

'Well, to get adopted, maybe I didn't have one. Not one that would have acknowledged me anyway. Jeez! I've only had an hour or so to think about it. It's more my Mom that I wonder about. I mean, you don't have to look too far to find a thousand reasons for not being able to raise a kid.'

'The golden band,' said Scoot, dreamily. 'I don't never want to father a child I don't know about.'

'Scoot, you're no more than fourteen years old.' I snorted at how stupid I sounded. This evening I'd talked to Scoot more like he was me than anyone else.

'Don't come the wise big sister with me,' said Scoot, 'I've had offers.'

'Sure you have, bro,' I said, and sneaked another cigarette. Clearly tonight had nothing to do with sleeping. I'd go back in the house and corner Mom and find out what the hell she'd been mickey-mousing around with all my life. No wonder she'd always gone dead when I asked her about my birth! She hadn't even been there! I'd grown up in a house of strangers, and there was some sorting out to do.

'Night, bro,' I said, turning myself upright. 'Let your old sis down, huh?'

'Sure thing, Monica,' said Scoot, grinning. 'Come up 'n see me some time, hey?'

'Aren't you goin back to the house?'

'The hell am I! I sleep out here most nights. Nobody seems to give a damn,' said Scoot, stretching. 'Hey, Monica, I'm really sorry about the guy you were in love with. Maybe he'll write.'

He? Of course. What else?

I climbed down the ladder and back into the yard. Now the sky had turned white and turquoise by the horizon. The stars were bleeding away. It was only hours short of a Disney sunrise. Tennessee Tex was soft-shoe shuffling around with 'Delta Dawn' in the house, and the lights seemed uncommonly bright. Pop was slumped over the table, beating out of time, and his lop-sided grin took me in.

'You missed the wedding party leaving. Hey, baby, got a kiss for your old Pop?'

'Thank you, no,' I said, and went into the kitchen, as he chuckled like he thought he knew something. Mom was sitting by the table, and her eyes raked my face as I stood facing her.

'Find yourself a beau, Monica?' she said, smiling, shaking her head like, you know, *kids*.

'I have to talk to you,' I said.

'Can't it wait till morning?' she smiled, all bleary, weary, put her head on her arms and fell asleep.

'It is morning,' I said.

3

I went upstairs and lay on my bed to wait out the next day. Some time later I was woken by Mom saying *Willard, for the love of God!* kind of urgent and anxious like she'd woken from a bad dream, then giggling real high like she was delighted about something. Then I heard Pop sort of snorting and groaning and Mom gasping out loud, crying out yes, yes, yes YES! like an animal goaded beyond bearing. Oh God, they were . . . *doing it.* I'd seen dogs do it in the street, and in the schoolyard we sniggered about fucking. I never had thought of Mom and Pop . . . doing it. A loving act between married couples, our biology teacher had said, all Miss Prim in her starched white coat, while we blushed and tried to look blasé over cross-section diagrams of the human reproductive organs. I closed my eyes and put the pillow over my ears. How could she let *him* do it to her?

I was first up around noon the next day. I stacked a few dishes, then thought why the hell should I. Let the real Robinsons clear up their own trash. I set myself up on the porch with a can of beer and a squashed packet of Marlboros I'd found on the floor. Mom would see me like she'd never seen me before. *WHAT THE HELL YOU THINK YOU'RE DOING SITTING ROUND LIKE SOME SLUT?* I'd stop her in her tracks, just say real cool: *Just who the hell do you think you're talking to? I'm not your daughter.*

But the beer was flat and sour and the paper was split on all but three of the Marlboros. I ground out the last butt and sat and stared around. Today we'd talk about It, and maybe they'd tell me how it happened I was the last to know about being adopted when Pop saw fit to blab it around to strangers. He could have told anyone fool enough to buy him a drink, any time he took off on a jag, any place he happened to break down in the whole county.

I heard someone coming downstairs. Mom? I walked back indoors to face her. But it was Pop, still fully dressed, unshaven, smiling like he was proud of himself and shaking all the bottles on the table for dregs. I wouldn't lower myself to share words with him.

'How's about a coffee for your old Pop, baby?'

I went back to sitting on the porch.

Pop's feet did an indignant shuffle at the back of me.

'I said, gal, how's about a coffee? Huh? 'Samatter with you? You been struck deaf and dumb?'

I mouthed into the dirt: 'You are not my Pop and I don't have to speak to you again for the rest of my life.'

He snorted and stomped like a weak man, and weak that he was, he backed down.

'Waaall, lookie here, my baby gal got herself a hangover, wouldn't ya know it! Pop'll fix the coffee.'

He stopped and turned at the door.

'Hey–eeey! I got it. You got yourself a beau, girl! Goddamn! You can't sit there all day with moonlight in your eyes! I'll fix my little girl a coffee and we'll set like grown-ups and have us a little chat.'

Well, Pop had himself a little chat while my coffee cooled on the porch-boards. I learnt a lot from Pop. Like how a girl has to be careful with young men, yessir, and he should know. A girl can lose her name quicker than a rabbit. And once a girl had lost her name, what man would touch her? Lost her name. Like he'd given me his name. Oh, men were something else, screwing up women's lives. Course, said Pop, engaged couples were different, but I wouldn't be thinking about a ring yet awhile. No sir, girls had a rough time of it, what with all looking so pretty and men being men, but he'd stand by me and see me right, just like he'd done with Rosemarie. He told me in a kind of guilty boast that Harry Welch would be farming the lower 40 acres now, it was a gentlemen's agreement. Not that I was to think less of Rosemarie or Billy Bob on account of the new arrangements, mind, it was all fair and square between our families.

Now those 40 acres just happened to be the one good piece of our land. Sold to the man with the reluctant bridegroom for a son! No wonder the wedding party had been whipped up so quick. No wonder Rosemarie had been so glad about it all. She'd 'saved her name' and drawn herself a real prize – a lifetime with Billy Bob Welch!

I learnt a lot about Pop while he rambled on, kind of nervous when I wouldn't say a word back to him. I just sat there daring him to get real mad at me. He couldn't.

Finally he started apologising about was I offended by him being a little merry the night before? Had he said something he shouldn't have? Done something he shouldn't have done? He looked mightily relieved when we heard Mom. She stood in the doorway, her hair all round her face.

'Hey, Kathereen!' he said anxiously, 'I been having a little conversation with Monica here, but maybe she needs a woman's touch, heh heh, I been doing most of the talking.'

All, I told the bleached knot of wood at my feet.

'So you both just sitting out here having a chat when there's enough pots and dishes and glasses to stack and clean from here to Christmas? Willard Robinson, I swear your tongue runs on wheels!'

She leaned on his shoulder and sat down with us, looking kind of pretty and pleased at Pop, and pulling her face right in for me.

'Honey, I'll get us more coffee,' said Pop, scrambling upright.

'Tuck your shirt in,' Mom threw over her shoulder. She sat, twisting her hair round and pulling it into a band, all strained and hard like it was most days.

'What's eating you, Monica?' she said. 'I guess you've learnt how it is with drinking now, and none too soon. Pop said you'd found yourself a beau, honey, come and tell Mom all about it.'

I looked at her under my elbow. *You're not my mother* died on my lips. I looked back at the dirt between my feet. Pop came hustling out with a tray and the coffee-pot and a paper rose in a blurred glass.

'Willard, you big fool,' said Mom, but it was more like a caress.

I waited till he'd fixed their coffee, tipped mine away and poured some fresh and sat beside me and Mom.

'You said,' I started, gazing at the lazy curl of steam from my cup, 'You were talking to Billy Bob's Pop last night. Something you said to him.'

'I talked a blue streak to Harry last night. I guess we set the world to rights one way and another. Jeez, Monica, baby, I don't recollect much, to tell you the God's honest truth.'

'Me and your Pop are too old to play guessing games, Monica. What did he say?' This was Mom like I knew her, tough, no messing round.

'He said how you and him adopted me in England.'

'*He's* your Pop, Monica. Don't speak about him in that tone, madam.'

'Well? Why didn't you tell me before? How come I have to hear about it by – accident? If I hadn't just been sitting by him and Harry last night I could have gone my whole life without knowing. Didn't you think I just might be the first to tell? For Chrissake, Mom!'

'You mind your mouth, Monica! Cussing your Mom!' Pop, spluttering.

'I asked you a question,' I said, with a white-hot rage that scared me.

'You ain't too big to whup.' Pop, blustering.

'Hush up, Willard. Of course we should have told you, Monica. But the time never seemed right. Of all the days, to pick the day after your sister's wedding!'

'It was no choice of mine,' I said, real low and even.

'God's sake, Monica! When you were a little girl, you were just one of our kids, and seeing you play along with Rosemarie and Scoot, it didn't seem right to burden you with the idea. Then you were all at school, and Rosemarie so proud of her little sister, then you so pleased to be showing Scoot around – my little brother – I guess I was just waiting for the right time and it never came. I'm real sorry you had to hear it like that. Willard, you got a lot to answer for.'

'Hell, Kathereen,' Pop whined in a don't-blame-me, injured voice, 'How was I to know? You shoulda said something to me last night, Monica, not run off to the fields with some boy!'

'You didn't see me when you were talking. Who's to say you'd hear me if I spoke to you? And I didn't run off to the fields with some boy. I damn near walked out of here. Maybe I should have done.'

'God's sake, child,' said Mom, and wrapped her wiry arms round me. 'Have you ever lacked for love? I've loved you like my own. You always were my own child, anyway. You were so tiny when I got you. There was no difference between you and the other two.'

'I know you've always loved me,' I said into her wrapper, 'but there is a difference. Hell, he said it all last night. I don't even look like you.'

Mom rocked me to and fro and called me baby. I felt her chin move in my hair and she said something to Pop. Whatever it was, he left the porch.

I pulled away from Mom. Nice and all, but I had this core of anger sitting inside me that no hug could touch. I felt like I'd been living a lie, being loyal to Pop, gritting my teeth for years about the fool way he was, punching out kids sneering at the Robinson farm, holding my head high when I knew folks were casting charitable looks our way, pretending that it suited me fine to have everything shoddy and second-hand. For nothing. For some bum who wasn't even my real Pop.

'You got to understand your Pop,' said Mom.

So. Understand? Him?

'Your Pop was never made for farming. He ran away from it all when he joined the Air Force. I've never seen a finer man in a uniform, Monica. I was working in a store in Baltimore when I met him. He walked in one afternoon like he could buy the whole shop, and drove me mad wanting to look at silk blouses. Finally it was closing time, and he'd bought nothing. Then he said he'd been pestering me so I'd have a date with him. And I did. Turned out he was going overseas the next week, so I married him. Monica, you should have known him then! We'd walk into a bar, and in five minutes he'd have the whole place dancing! And he never looked at another girl but me. You'll find out how rare that is. And what with travelling and Rosemarie, it wasn't till we got to England that I started worrying about his drinking. I was desperate to have another child, he was spoiling Rosemarie so much. And the doctor had said I wasn't likely to have another. So I decided we'd adopt. He'd been so lovely when Rosemarie came along.'

So I was supposed to be a sobering influence.

'Well, honey, we went everywhere. It's not easy to adopt. You have to fill in forms, get interviewed, get turned down, reapply, more forms – I'd near given up, when they called and said there was a baby we could come and have a look at. And there you were, Monica, lying in a high hard cot, so pale and so tiny. I picked you up, and you looked straight at me. I looked straight at you and you kind of snuggled up and fell straight asleep like you were comfortable with me. Your Pop couldn't get away from the base to come with me, so we rode back in a cab, just you and me. And ever since then you've been my baby.'

So he couldn't even be bothered to come and get his new daughter. Jesus! How I hated that man, no Pop of mine. But she, my Mom, she'd stand by him just as crazy as Tammy Wynette, she'd make any excuse in the book for him. And it just wasn't good enough for me.

'So what happened to the Air Force?'

'Child, you got daggers in your voice!' Mom warned. 'We've always put you kids first, and we got a wire to say your grandpa had died and left everything to Willard. It's no life for children, traipsing round the globe. So we came back here. And we've worked ever since to give you a good life.'

'*You* have. I know that.'

'Your Pop's sweated blood over the land. There's a word getting lost here, Monica. Gratitude. Your Pop's a good man and I won't hear different. It's not every man would take on a child that's not his own, give them his name and bring them up like family.'

I was choked. Seemed like the whole damn world revolved round Willard Robinson. I had to *understand* him, and now I had to be *grateful* as well. Did I ask them to pick me out? Jesus! To think of me lying there, for them to come and look at me like I was goods in a store – 'Oh, yes, we'll have this one, could you have it wrapped? Gee, I just hope my husband likes it! He's such a busy man!'

But I couldn't say any of this to Mom.

'You got any papers about me? I mean, like, with my real name on?'

Mom stared at me and her mouth went into a tight line.

'Your real name is Monica Robinson. And don't you forget it. I got things to do. It wouldn't hurt you to lend a hand.'

She left me, banging the screen door behind her.

We all met again at supper. It was always a silent meal, but today the silence hissed around like static on the radio when the station shuts down for the night. Scoot and Pop never raised their eyes from their plates. Mom passed dishes round and when her eyes met mine they were dark and fiery.

I figured she'd left me with a question. There had to be papers of some sort somewhere round the house. And I had a right to see them.

Me and Scoot cleared the table. We usually washed and dried in silence, there being nothing to say. Today Scoot threw out, casually:

'You want to play cards? Over there?'

Why the hell not. We slipped out of the back door. I felt a little wary, like maybe I'd spilled too much the night before. But Scoot didn't make any assumptions about us suddenly being best buddies, just sloshed out a drink, a cigarette and dealt just like any good old boy. I went off to bed after a few games, tiptoeing past the living-room door where I could hear Mom talking to Pop.

'Well, let's hope she's happy, Willard.'

Happy? How could I be happy with this charade?

'Yup, Kathereen, we gave her a good send-off.'

Oh, so they weren't even talking about me. After all that, they were just sitting pretty back-patting themselves over Rosemarie. It was as if nothing had happened, we'd goof around from one day to the next and just forget that Monica *ain't ours*, that Monica *don't favour neither one of us*. I'd never felt so alone before. Mom had Pop, for what it was worth, Rosemarie had Billy Bob, Harry Welch had our 40 acres, and even Scoot had his own place, and dreams besides.

I had nothing.

Well, I had good grades in English, and tomorrow was school and I'd be out of the house. But school meant no more Joanne Lee Hunter, my sun and moon, my rising star. I'd be better off dead, or disappeared somewhere under the clouded, starless sky.

4

'Hey, some party at your place Saturday!'
The voice whined its way through the catatonic fog around me. A face distorted with gum, hair plastered back, and a sweatshirt saying STUD were jiggling from one foot to the other in front of me.

'I wuz gonna git a dance with you, but y'disappeared. Y'goin' with anyone?'

I walked through him.

'Hey, Monica, what'd he say?'

'Who?'

'*Him*. Dean John Welch. He's real sweet on you! Ever since Rosemarie and Billy Bob got hitched. He's been *looking* at you since Monday.'

Oh, that'd be cute! Two sisters and two brothers getting married. Pop could give away the upper pasture to get rid of me.

'Well, he can look elsewhere.'

'Monica! He's so cute! Maybe he'll ask you to the Prom!'

'I feel a lot better knowing that, Sue Ann. It's been preying on my mind.'

'God, you're so sarcastic, Monica! He's only trying. But I forgot. Monica Robinson only needs the company of a good book. You hafta start thinking about boys, Monica. Charles Dickens ain't going to warm your bed.'

'I gotta go,' I said. Jeez, Sue Ann was getting to be a pain. Ever since she'd been dating Ted Bulstrode she'd got the same terminal symptoms as Rosemarie. Giggles. Make-up. A new outfit every day. Mondays filled with Ted said, Ted did, me and Ted had such a good time at the weekend! She used to have plans to look after kids on a world cruise ship. Now her horizons had closed in around a board house, an eye-level grill with a timing bleep and a bathroom suite in Eastern Rose.

But I had taken my life into my own hands. Tonight I was starting at Sam's cafe/bar, six through eleven, Wednesday till Friday, and all day Saturday. Sam's window always had a sign 'Help Wanted', and I'd shocked him into saying yes by walking in the Monday after the wedding, all ready to start. Pop had offered to pick me up, seeing as it meant he had a reason for coming out to the bar. I had never intended to take another thing or favour from Pop, but I figured it was a fair trade, his boozing for my freedom. I should be able to put away near 40 bucks a week. I was aiming at 2,000. Then I'd split. Mom had pursed her lips when I told her I had a job, then shrugged and said at least I could pay for my own schoolbooks that way; she'd started work at fifteen, done her no harm. And maybe wiping tables would give me ideas about making myself useful around the place.

I pushed open the doors to Sam's.

'Nice and early! We're kinda quiet now, Monica. I'll show you the place. Now, honey, here's your overall.'

He handed me a blue-check nylon tube, with a lace ruff at the sleeves and neck. There was a pink heart to sit over my left nipple.

'The girls usually embroider their own name there, honey lamb. My wife, Doris, had the idea. Adds a bit of character, y'know. Gives th'old boys something to call you, besides.'

'Sam. I can't wear this.'

'Whuh? It's to protect your clothes. Grease and stuff.'

'Sam, I don't give a damn about a little grease on my clothes, but I can't wear a thing like this. Look at me!'

I pulled it over my head. I could see myself distorted every way eight times in the chrome over the bar. I looked like an understudy for Baby Jane.

'Yeah, yeah,' said Sam. 'So you don't like the overall. OK. But the boys do like a frill or two – y'know?'

'Tell you what – I'll get a frilled shirt – OK?'

It was OK. I dived down the street, and picked myself a Mississippi gambler number I'd been eyeing up for weeks in Miss Eliza's Quality Clothing Emporium. It was lilac sateen with rows of lace down the front, and a rat-tail leather bow at the neck.

'This garment ain't designed for womenfolk,' said Miss Eliza

28

nervously, as I checked myself out in the mirror. 'But I guess it'd be fancy dress for you young people.'

We young people blew our savings on the shirt, and blew Miss Eliza's mind by wearing it on the spot.

'See what I mean, Sam?'

'Gosh darn, you look real smart, Monica. Naw, you ain't the overall type.'

'Sam, I'm not the cabaret. I'm here to serve drinks.'

'Speaking of which, I always do say, when there's an occasion to celebrate, I'm the man to celebrate it in Style! This here's your first day at Sam's! We'll have us a little shot together before it gits lively. And I got me a piece of advice. I ain't fussed if the customers want to buy you drinks, shows they're having themselves a good time. But go easy. I had a girl here once, so purdy she got bought a drink for every table she served. She liked vodky. She never done a stroke after nine at night being as she was collapsed under a table. She brought the boys in all *right*! But damned if she kept 'em coming! What do you drink, Monica?'

'Beer,' I said, 'and – cocktails.'

I didn't feel I wanted to share the secret of the Scoot Deluxe. Sam knew everyone's business in What Cheer and was happy to mouth it around when he got merry.

'Stick to the beer, gal! Stick to the beer for everyday drinking. But they's only one way to celebrate!'

He fetched out an unlabelled bottle, and confided that it was bourbon like distilleries never get their hands on for all their greenbacks. No, sir, it was an old moonshine recipe, brewed up by his cousin out in the hills. It took my breath away. *Never give it to customers*, he warned, else they'll get sick at paying for the name brands.

Sam's stayed quiet till around eight, with just one or two locals loafing in to nurse a beer. Then a crowd of boys came in all together, oiled up and ready to swagger. They were the 'chance', Sam whispered, lotsa easy money – a gang of out-of-towners, paid by the day on a building development of Harry Welch's, and resented by all the neighbourhood. Harry Welch had a way of turning dirt into dollars overnight, but not being a What Cheer Boy born and bred, he had the darnedest time getting hands locally. His go-ahead city ways aroused suspicion;

his success aroused growling envy. Ours was nicknamed the Show-Me county, old country boys slit-eyed and ready to spit at new-fangled ways of business. And how they did get riled when a city boy like Harry showed them good and proper every time!

'Well, howdy little lady, damned if it ain't good to see a woman in this place! What's yuh name?'

'Monica,' I said, little lady, for Chrissake! 'What can I get you?'

'Yeep, hoop! Hey, Slim, what can the little lady git us?'

I was facing a line of faces identical aside from a millimetre or two in the placing of eyes and noses and the angles at which their lips were leering. You are a woman and I'm a blood-raw man.

'Waaa–ll, now, what can you git us? Hey, Grady, hi hi hi!' said the second mouth, lurking in its sparse beard.

'Maybe you'd like a ratburger,' I muttered. Two of the faces heard and laughed themselves sick.

'Whuh she say? Whuh you say? Huh? Whuh you say, gal?'

'I'm waiting for your order,' I said.

'Gwan, you're beat. Six cold beers, Monica,' said another mouth, grinning.

They jostled over to a table, with Slim and Grady still hollering 'whuh she say?' Sam told me I'd handled them well. They were the bunch who'd gotten my predecessor triple vodkas just for the fun of seeing her fall on her butt.

'Go and see to that table,' said Sam. I looked over. Christ Almighty! Reverend Taylor Hadley was sitting chatting away with Miss Margaret Courtland, like they were in some restaurant in a movie, not slumming it at Sam's. I gave them a menu, and Miss Courtland arched her eyebrows at me.

'I didn't know you worked here, Monica. You know Reverend Hadley? We have a discussion group on Wednesdays and come in here afterwards.'

'Yes,' said Reverend Hadley, with the glass-eyed grin that had got him named the Goldfish of God, 'I must be seen among my people, like the Man Upstairs said. Thank you, Monica, was it? We'll call you over when we're ready.'

I left them talking the Spirit of the Living God and steak or ribs. I felt humiliated, tell the truth. What would Margaret

Courtland think of her 'A' student waiting tables, and being hailed as sweetheart by a table of rednecks? I clenched my teeth.

'Reverend always do have himself a pitcher of Mariposa Valley Red. There's times when Miss Courtland will have a sherry before the meal – tell you what, Monica, set up a tray and take it over. Make a good impression.'

I set the tray on the table.

'Sam said to bring this over.'

'Well, well, Margaret, my dear, we must be becoming regulars! Thank you so much. And now we'll order,' said Reverend Taylor Hadley like he was about to spread the Word of God.

'We'll have ribs and fries and onion rings. Mmmwah!' he kissed his pudgy fingers. 'And a salad of the finest. We put ourselves in your hands, Monica. Marg – Miss Courtland has been telling me that you're a most promising student. Keep it up!'

He lashed a half-gallon of red wine into his glass, clinked with Miss Courtland's pale schooner and gulped.

'Ribs and fries and onion rings and a side salad,' I said to Sam. He hollered through the hatch at Blackfoot Pete, the chef.

I was only vaguely aware of the two of them for the rest of the evening. Folk filled the place around nine; around ten the town drunks came shuffling in with Pop on their heels. He got himself a line of beers swaggering about his li'l girl gettin' growed and having herself a job. We bumped home in the truck. What he said I don't know, being as I'd decided to go deaf while he was talking, but I knew I was ten bucks into leaving. Plus the fifty I'd rolled from him. Minus the twenty-two I'd blown on the shirt.

Mom had a hot supper waiting for me, but I'd eaten around nine-thirty. Pop found his way upstairs and I sat toying with the food, with Mom over the other side of the table.

'First day at work, huh?' she said.

'Mm.'

'Monica – what we talked about at the weekend. We've always loved you like our own, you know.'

She was ready to talk. But I was not.

'Gee, Mom,' I said, 'I'm just not hungry.'

'Well, good night then,' she said bleakly. It was a declaration of cold war.

'Night.'

The next day was not so simple. Miss Courtland told me to come see her after school. At her house. My heart was thumping as I got to her door. My grades were good enough, weren't they? I'd had a hard time with the last essay: Symbolism in Jane Austen. I hadn't been happy with the nit-picky little world of *Pride and Prejudice*, and couldn't put my heart into it. It was a helluva title, but I couldn't get involved with all that prissy wooing. I liked guts, like you got in *Wuthering Heights* and such. Whatever Miss Courtland had to say, I had to be at the cafe by six.

'Oh, I'm glad you came. Would you like a cup of tea?'

'Yes, please.'

Miss Courtland had the cutest thinnest china I'd ever seen. Like varnished eggshells with gold rims and sprays of violets. Maybe my real mother did this sort of thing, it was so English, afternoon tea and dainty biscuits.

'When did you start work at the cafe, Monica?'

'Just this week.'

'I hope it's not going to interfere with your studies,' she said.

'Hell, no. Excuse me. I mean, no. I do most of my studying weekends anyway.'

'And are you going to work "weekends"?' she said, in a tone of soft accusation.

'Only Saturdays. I got Sundays.'

'A student like you shouldn't be wasting her time in Sam's Cafe. You could go far if you applied yourself.'

'Well, I guess I need the money,' I mumbled, noticing the streaks of tea down the side of my cup. I also noticed how Margaret swallowed without making any sound at all. I felt like a goddam slob!

'I wondered if that was the reason. I do understand. I took a Saturday job at Woolworth's when I was your age. But late nights during the week are another thing altogether. I was going to ask you something. What time do you finish at Sam's?'

'About eleven.'

'And then there's the drive home. You have to get up early for the bus as well. I think it might be best if you stayed in town

32

on Wednesdays and Thursdays. I have a spare room. Would you like to do that? I'd ask your parents, of course.'

Would I like to do that? Hell, yes!

'That's very kind of you.'

'No,' said Miss Courtland, 'Not kind. I can see that you have a lot of academic potential. You could get to college. I'd like to do what I can to help. Talk to your parents and tell me what they say. I'll telephone them if there are any problems.'

Well, upon my word!

I spent the evening waiting tables and turning this over in my mind. It made sense. I was tickled pink, tell the truth. But there was no saying what way Mom would jump. She could be mighty awkward when she chose, especially since the wedding. It had always been up to her to make most decisions in our house, and what I had to avoid was a flat No. A threatening 'we'll see' or 'maybe' was what I got most times. She never once committed herself to *Yes*, and then she'd say she'd told me so and what did I expect. Twice Sue Ann had asked me to stay over for a party, and that had been a No I'd been fool enough to question. Which meant I didn't even go to the party. *A decent girl sleeps in her own bed nights.* And I knew Pop would be against it, being as how he'd lose his excuse for coming into Sam's that way. But that should work for me from Mom's point of view. And just what could she find against Miss Courtland? She was respectable, a church-going teacher, and Mom could take the credit for me being a good student, besides. Still, I was uneasy.

I mentioned it to Pop on the way home, testing out ways to put it to Mom.

'You ain't turning into no bookworm, gal?' he said anxiously. 'You oughtta be thinkin' about a beau. Ain't no Robinsons been to college. We always been on the land.'

Well, I was no Robinson and I'd heard it from his lips. I held my breath so my ears rang deaf against any other foolishness he might throw my way. I'd missed supper at Sam's so that Mom wouldn't be offended by me not eating supper at home.

'Knew you wouldn't stomach that cafe food long,' she said flatly. 'Well, I ain't fixed you nothing, being as you wouldn't eat nothing yesterday. I got enough to do without kids turning up their noses at good nourishment. Fix yourself some bread and ham, if you're needing food in your ungrateful belly.'

It was a bad time: Mom was elbow deep in mending, a task she did with religious hatred and nagged me for not learning how.

'Mom,' I said.

She snapped thread against her teeth and stared at me.

'You got something to say, speak plain.'

'Well,' I should have left it be, but it was too late. 'You know I'm working at the cafe Wednesdays and Thursdays?'

'You want me to say "yes" – course I know. You been bragging about nothing else for the past week.'

'Well, Miss Courtland – the English teacher – has offered to have me stay over with her those two nights, seeing as it's late.'

She knotted the thread.

'Is that OK with you? It would mean Pop wouldn't have to come out to pick me up those nights.'

She picked up a dull grey button.

'That's true.'

I breathed too soon.

'It's also true that you are the idlest body I've ever seen for a growing girl. Oh, you can work when it suits you. School learning, waiting tables for money. But I've yet to see you raise a hand round your own home without me reminding you. I get so tired asking you to do things, Monica, seems it'd be easier to do them myself. And I do. I do every piece of work around the house so you can play the fine lady at that damn school. And you don't have a shred of gratitude. And just who is this Miss Courtland?' she said with a vicious sneer. She knew damn well who Miss Courtland was. Last semester she'd smiled at my report and said at least there was someone recognised Robinsons had brains. I kept my voice light.

'She's the English teacher, Mom. You know. The first one to give me As. She says I could get into college if I worked.'

'Seems to me you're getting ideas,' she said menacingly, twirling the button down the thread. 'College! Whatever next for my high-flying daughter? And just who is supposed to foot the bill for your fancy ideas? I never took a nickel off my Mom after I was thirteen years old, and here you are, nearly seventeen, your Pop and me scraping to keep you at school, fools that we are. Some girls your age are running their own homes and would be shamed to ask their folks for money. And now it's college. You'll be twenty and more before you're earning your keep.'

Her needle stabbed in and out of the shirt cuff and she twisted thread round the back of the button tight enough to strangle.

'Get yourself to bed, madam. I don't need fool ideas from you.'

I got to bed. She hadn't said Yes, but she hadn't said No, either.

It seemed I'd only just fallen asleep, twitching awake over would she, wouldn't she, when all at once Mom hammered into the room, ripped the covers off me, and stood by the bed in her wrap with her hair and her eyes wild. I wasn't hardly awake and she was hissing at me like a nest of snakes.

'You can get up of a morning, lying idle and waiting for the bus to school like a fine lady! You think there's nothing to do in the house? Nothing you'd stoop to soil your fancy hands with? I'll show you what work is, girl, and more's the shame I never showed you earlier. You wouldn't come at me with your high-falutin notions if you'd ever done a stroke in your life! Get your body dressed and get downstairs! NOW!'

She screamed the last work and tore from the room. By the windowlight I could tell it wasn't even sun-up. She'd gone crazy. I was terrified and flung my clothes on any how.

Downstairs she had the kettle and three big pans steaming on the stove. She stood glaring at me over a pile of the week's clothes slap-bang in the middle of the floor.

'Now,' she panted, tugging at shirts and sheets, 'I'm gonna teach you what a woman's work is. Catch the end of this!'

The sheet whiplashed across my head, and as I caught it and fell, it ripped across.

'Hah!' she screeched. 'There's my daughter! Don't know the meaning of work and don't know the value of money! Just rips up good linen to amuse herself! That sheet comes outta your wages. And you can sew it across besides. Get that pan of water!'

I poured the water into the wash copper. Mom never would hear of an automatic washing machine, even if Pop had the money to get one, which he did about once a year. *Elbow-grease and good eyesight cleans clothes better than any blind paddle*, she said. *You want my family to walk around in machine-washed clothes?* Yes, Mom, no, Mom. None of us said a word when she was in that mood. I got to my feet and sorted the clothes.

We washed and scrubbed, and wrung and hung in silence. I swear to God I thought she was capable of killing me. All of a sudden, when my arms were wet and red and fit to fall off, she sat down at the table. She smiled in this bright, polite way. And said wasn't I about ready for some coffee, cuz she could surely use a cup? I felt goose-bumps on my shoulders. I made the coffee and slid a look at the hall clock. It was six-thirty. We must have been up since five.

'You done good, Monica,' she said, in a strange voice, kind of soft and high. 'That's the wash done. Tomorrow we can get the brasses polished. Now you got the notion of work, I can get this house looking like a body puts some care into it.'

I sipped the coffee and didn't dare look at her. She'd gone crazy. Crazy, like mad old Lou in What Cheer, who wandered the streets cursing everybody out, throwing hunks of wood at cars one minute, and chasing kids down the street to buy them candy the next. Mom had warned me about mad old Lou – stay out of her way, child, she ain't right in the head. And now I was sitting across the table from someone gone screwy, drinking coffee like nothing was wrong, and this screwball just happened to be my Mom.

I had about abandoned my slow savings plan, and decided to take my chances thumbing my way out of this bug-house show, when Pop came stumbling into the kitchen in his pyjamas.

'Lord God,' he said, 'I smelt the coffee in my sleep, Kathereen! What're you all up for so early?'

He was smiling like an ugly dog that knows it's going to get whupped for something, and is just hoping against the odds you might think it's cute enough to leave be.

'There's coffee in the pot,' said Mom in her normal voice. 'Me and Monica been doing the work that needs doing. Seeing as how she's going gallivanting evenings these days.'

Gallivanting! Pop sat at the table waiting for the axe to fall.

'Seems we got ourselves a college girl here, Willard. She's got herself a teacher thinks a lot of her. So she'll be staying in town

Wednesdays and Thursdays now. She don't need her Pop to give her a ride no more. Hah!'

Pop's nodding was like a desperate tailwag.

'Of course,' said Mom, standing up over us, 'we'll just have to see how this smart teacher takes to her smart pupil once she knows the slut's ways she's gotten into.'

I said nothing. *She'd said YES!*

'You can fix breakfast now, the pair of you. I'm going to get myself cleaned up for the rest of the day. My work's only just got started.'

Her parting shot came as I heard the bus and escaped for the door.

'Hard work taken your voice away, miss? Blood will tell!'

All the way to school I sat saying in my head all the things I didn't have the guts to say aloud to her. How dare she fling that at me! I didn't even know what my blood was, *she* hadn't even told me. Scoot took one look at my face and slouched to another seat, sprawling with his cap over his face.

My mind was racing. If I let her know how I minded, teeth-grinding the words back, blood-red rage pounding in my head, she'd know to use it again. I'd seen her do it to Pop often enough, goading him about drink, only then I'd been on her side.

I hated her for acting like a crazy woman. I hated her because she was my Mom that I'd loved all my life, goddam it, and now she'd thrown the same scorn at me she always threw at him, and hadn't I always been on her side, hadn't I? And I hated her because there wasn't a damn thing I could do about any of it.

5

Suddenly it was lunchtime: I'd spent the morning in a turmoil of anger and fear about Mom. Most of school I just sat through, clock-watching lessons, the summer heat or the winter heating drawing my eyelids closed, tired voices doling out facts and figures for us to copy down and regurgitate for exams. Friday afternoons at school were the best bit of the week: we had Miss Courtland, and I was one of her best students. At least someone thought I was OK – OK enough even to have me stay with her. I never was aware of time passing with Miss Courtland. From start to finish there was this atmosphere of excitement and discovery. Everything was *fascinating*. She had this marvellous English voice and she talked like a book. She wasn't beautiful, but her face was so alive and mobile and intelligent, even the studs in the class conceded she was a damn fine-looking woman. And their pin-ups were all petite, blonde, lip-glossed and cute. Most tall women get a stoop to shrink themselves into something conventional, but Miss Courtland stood proud as the figurehead of a ship. Her thick hair was flung into a bun high on the back of her head in a glossy tortoiseshell slide. She looked you right in the eye when she spoke, and listened to every word you said.

'English Literature is my passion,' she told us, and what could we do but follow her like the Pied Piper?

We were thousands of miles and a century away from her world of books, but she brought each dead author to life with a gutsy phrase or ridiculous anecdote. To this day I have a picture of Wordsworth's sister scrabbling through his waste-bin for crumpled shreds of genius, blind John Milton ruling the roost from his sanctimonious study. She didn't like Milton and neither did any of us.

'You'll be pleased to know this,' she said with a wicked laugh, after we'd laboured through the endless mire of *Paradise Lost*: 'On his death-bed, John Milton begged his long-suffering daughters to burn the manuscript. Unfortunately for you, his wishes were disregarded!'

I printed her every word on my mind, as she drew me into this new land. I loitered in smoggy gaslit Dickensian streets; I strode the bleak crags of Yorkshire with an icy wind on my cheeks. I walked the heaving deck of a continental ferry, looking my last on the white cliffs of Dover, bound for a ghostly Europe that I had never seen. She showed us pictures of Victorian London, Edwardian Paris; delicate engravings of crinolined ladies simpering from a brougham, gentlemen in tight pants smirking and twirling their fine moustaches. On Fridays, if we had finished our assignments, she'd read to us for the last part of the afternoon. Even now when I pick up a book, I can hear her voice bringing life and breath and colour to a sentence. Then she'd snap the book shut and stare at us with her bright grey eyes.

'And what do you think happens next?'

Even the brain-dead in the class would be straining to say something, and she'd treat any answer with interest and respect, refashioning any awkward phrase into a thing of beauty. She made you feel you mattered.

So I was breathing easy as we waited for her in class that afternoon. She came in with her restless stride, but her face was set and distant. She handed back our work in silence. Normally she'd find a nice thing to say about most of the papers, and everybody would groan good-humouredly as she read out the best, which was mostly me and Zip Singer. Zip was OK for a boy, he'd been punched out and jeered at all through school until the autumn semester he came back a good six inches taller than any other kid. He wore glasses and was thin as a rake, given to blushing if you spoke to him direct. His folks lived on the outskirts of town, his father was a piano-tuner and Zip played the violin. All the meathead jocks let him alone now – he didn't fight, play baseball, drink, curse, gamble, chase girls or show any other sign of manhood. He spent lunchtime and after school in the library, hunched over a pile of books, making neat pencilled notes from each one. They called him freak and professor, but Zip never let on that he heard. I looked over to see how he was taking Miss Courtland and her haughty silence. He was beet-red. Jeez! She hadn't even given his paper back!

'I had hoped to be able to teach you something about Literature,' said Miss Courtland finally. 'I have been pleased by your work so far, so much so that I introduced you to my favourite writer, Jane Austen. It was my mistake. No one in this class has taken the trouble to appreciate *Pride and Prejudice*; not one of you has shown the slightest sign of interest or intelligence in your essays, apart from Zachary Singer.'

Zip blushed crimson and pushed his glasses up his nose. I felt like dirt.

'Try not to cry, Monica,' hissed Sue Ann. There were snickers all round me.

'If you would give me your attention, I will read Zachary's essay. You may learn something,' said Miss Courtland. Her words froze me where I sat, in some cold outer circle of her disapproval.

Zip's essay was something else. He sounded like he'd enjoyed the damn book, and talked about Regency society and values, referring to contemporary authors, politicians, land reform and a whole heap else. When I did an essay, I got taken over by the book and wrote like crazy. It all just came to me, and Miss Courtland's margin comments were usually highly complimentary. I could never have researched like Zip. Shit! I just wasn't a serious student. So much for college. Our class was split between the high-flyers, the hard-working middle-of-the-roaders – mostly girls – and the delinquent deadheads. So, be a deadhead and hang around with the gang? I'd never settle for the mediocre middle way. That was Sue Ann and Ted Bulstrode, engagement rings and mortgages.

For the rest of the awful afternoon we sat and rewrote the assignment, with Miss Courtland walking round, throwing out comments. I'd never seen her in this mood before. Finally the bell rang and everybody shuffled their books together and slunk out of the room.

'Monica.'

I went over to her desk.

'Well,' she said, 'what happened to you?'

Aside from my Mom going crazy and me flipping in my best subject and feeling like I'd be better dead . . .

'I dunno. I just couldn't get into it.'

'You look exhausted. A poor essay isn't the end of the world. Although I had expected more from you. You can't rely on a good turn of phrase to get you through. You're lucky with words, but you need to put a lot more time into solid research – back up your intuition with facts. You'll never be as meticulous as Zachary Singer, but Zachary Singer doesn't have your spark. Learn from him: a good college will need to know that you can apply yourself.'

I nodded. Any words would have brought out the tears. What a way to end the week.

'Anyway, the lecture's over,' she said. 'Did you ask your parents about staying with me?'

'Yes,' I said. 'It's OK with them.' If you still want me.

'Well, that's good. It will be nice to have company. Monica, what *is* the matter?'

I looked at her through a blur. I couldn't cope with the warmth in her voice, her clear strong gaze. Didn't she know I felt worse than dirt?

'For goodness' sake!' she said, 'whatever's wrong? Don't tell me Jane Austen and I have reduced *you* to tears!'

I couldn't say anything, just stood shaking and crying like I was five years old.

'You'd better come back for tea,' she said. 'You don't start your job until six, do you? Here – take my key and let yourself in. I've got to clear my desk in the staffroom, but I'll be home soon. Put the kettle on.'

I set my jaw to get by the crowd of meatheads lounging round the gates.

'Whassa matter, Monica?' jeered Henry Binnie, who acted like a leader on account of his brawn and brainlessness.

'You leave her be!' That was Dean John Welch, my acned knight in shining armour.

'I don't need your protection,' I told him. 'You got something to say, Henry? Huh?'

Henry had nothing to say to my face.

And so to Miss Courtland's. I opened the door and stepped inside. Her house was so quiet. There were books wall to wall, beautiful watercolours and Chinese plates. I felt like a house-breaker, walking through to the kitchen. She had a tea tray set for one, and I opened her cupboards to find myself a cup. I found rows of preserves marked in her stylish handwriting, with the date on matching labels with a fancy border. The china cupboard was stacked neatly, every cup and plate embellished with flowers or fruit. I thought of our house where every piece of china was old and ugly, but not too chipped to use; the huge jars and bottles of fruit and preserves Mom put up every autumn, turning the kitchen into a no-go area for two weeks while she boiled and strained until she was exhausted. Why didn't *she* label things and make them look special: *a body can see through glass, and I ain't got the time to do no fancy labels*, she'd say. And add a rider about gracious lady notions that were dreamed up by folks that had nothing better to occupy themselves with.

The kettle was polished copper and as I set it on the stove, I heard the front door.

'Oh, good, we're all organised,' said Miss Courtland. 'You go through and get comfortable.'

'Now,' she said, pouring tea, 'what's been happening?'

I felt kind of embarrassed at all that crying.

'Oh, I dunno.'

'Nonsense,' she said softly. 'You look white as a sheet. Something's happened. School? Home?'

So I told her about Mom last night and this morning. It sounded kind of trivial spoken out loud. I felt disloyal, too, and did my best to play it down.

'It's not so bad,' I finished. 'She'll get over it. Sorry.'

'You have nothing to be sorry about. Now, your mother's complaining that you don't help around the house. Do you?'

'I do a bit,' I said, 'only she always says she can do it better.'

'Well, I'm sure she can. She's had plenty of practice. Didn't your sister get married a couple of weeks ago? Did she do a lot round the house?'

'I guess so. She seemed to like it. Oh, Rosemarie's always been the one to help Mom. I used to help Pop, I guess.'

'So now your mother's missing Rosemarie and probably feeling old as well. You'll have to make up to her a bit. Don't worry. It's not the end of the world.'

It all sounded so sane the way she put it. I got a flashback to our kitchen this morning, when Mom was staring at me like she'd murder me. Maybe I was exaggerating.

'What about your father? We've never seen him at school apart from when your notorious brother has been playing up.'

'Oh, Scoot's OK,' I said. 'Pop's OK too. You know.'

'Was he in the cafe the other night?'

I blushed. Of course, she'd been there and seen Willard Robinson in all his boozing glory.

'What do they think about you going to college?'

'Pop thinks I should get myself a beau, and Mom thinks I'm getting fancy ideas. I don't think we've got the money.'

'All the more reason for the Zachary Singer approach to studying. You should go for a scholarship, Monica. I'm sure you could do it.'

Right at that moment I felt I could do nothing.

'I'd better be getting over to Sam's,' I said. 'Thanks.'

'Thanks nothing, as you Yankees say,' she smiled. 'I'll tell you what: I have the Christian Awareness discussion group on Wednesdays. Would you like to come?'

'I'm not much for church and stuff,' I mumbled.

'I think you need Jesus in your life,' she said, low and sincere, 'I'll pray for you. It'll be all right when you get home – your mother's probably more upset than you.'

I hadn't told her about Mom's parting scream: *Blood will tell!*

I hadn't told her I was not Monica Robinson, but some nameless person born to God knows who, God knows where.

'So, I'll be expecting you late on Wednesday. You could come over after school on Thursday before you start work, and I can try and persuade you of the merits of Jane Austen. Take care, Monica. Try to have a good weekend.' She squeezed my shoulder and I managed a smile.

On the way to Sam's I stopped by the general store to pick up a new sheet out of my dwindling capital. That should please Mom. Tomorrow morning I'd do out the kitchen before I went to work. Sunday I should study, but I could help her do the midday meal. I had no intention of giving her any reason to go wild at me. I could even study at lunchtimes at school. And it was only five days until Wednesday night.

I served the tables in a blur. Some asshole grabbed my arm.

43

'Do you ever smile, sweetheart? Give me a treat, crack your pretty face!'

I was more likely to crack his. It might look better that way.

'C'mon baby, it might never happen!'

And what if it already has?

'Honey, your Pop's over there!' said Sam, nudging me.

I looked over, ready to duck my eyes if he was facing this way. What! Mom was with him. She never went out with him! But here she was, smiling my way with her best dress on. Scoot was beside them, his hair all flattened over his scrubbed face. Harry Welch and his wife were sitting at the same table, beckoning me over. A real family get-together.

'Well, go and take their order, girl!'

I walked over, heart thumping.

'I thought I'd come and see for myself,' said Mom, her eyes searching my face. 'You look real smart, Monica. I thought you'd have an overall, but that is a very nice shirt.'

'I got the sheet,' I said. Goddammit! I'd spent an entire day of misery, sweating with fear about going home and now she wanted us to be cosy?

Her face darkened and she looked sad and tired. At once I was sorry.

'What can I get you?' I said quickly. 'Here's a menu.'

'I'm not hungry,' said Mom. 'You all order.' She wouldn't meet my eyes.

I took the order and walked away shaking. Blackfoot Pete was standing at the hatch, and scrawled down what I told him.

'And Pete,' I said, 'What do you give a lady to drink when she's feeling a bit old and sad and doesn't approve of alcohol?'

Pete scratched his jaw, and nodded to the moonshine stashed under the bar.

'Put in a load of ice, an orange twist and a squeeze of soda,' he said. 'Then she won't know why she's feeling good.'

I did just that, and set it with the beers in front of my folks.

'That's for you, Mom,' I said, 'It's mainly fruit and soda. On the house.'

Mom sipped and raised the glass to me with a little of her old fire.

'Waaall, she wouldn't do nothing special for her old Pop,' he whined, like he was heart-broken. 'No, sir, I have to pay for my drinks, just like I was anybody!'

'Willard, hush up!' said Mom.

If I'd had my way, he'd have been banned from Sam's let alone getting free drinks. As I moved round the room I could hear him telling anyone that would listen that I was his little girl and din' they grow up fast?

I was up first on Saturday, and did every fool thing I could think of in the kitchen, scrubbed the table, swept and washed the floor, scoured the pans so the outsides were shining. When I heard footsteps overhead I started on the breakfast, flinging a cloth on the table, cracking eggs and frying ham like Blackfoot Pete when there was a rush on. The kitchen looked a whole heap better: she'd have to be pleased about it.

'Lord,' said Mom, 'what's gotten into you?'

'Just felt like it,' I said with my back to her.

'Well, let's hope it's not a five-minute wonder. Put an apron on, Monica, you'll be all over grease and I ain't washing extra clothes for your careless ways,' said Mom, taking all the joy out of the day.

I served them breakfast and coffee. Pop was all ready to start blustering about a damn fine meal, but Mom picked at her food, *she'd* never fried an egg *that* way, never cut ham that way to fry, besides she never did relish a greasy meal to start the day with.

'Well, maybe you'll give me a hand to sort this kitchen before you go running off to that cafe,' she said.

'Well, I've done it,' I said. 'The floor, the table, the pots.'

'And what did you use on the table? Lord, girl, you have to wax a wooden table. Scrubbing's only the half of it. Washing tiles don't make a floor clean. You got to seal it, the amount of dirt gets traipsed through here! Monica, you have a lot to learn.'

I stared at my plate. She had that high, brisk tone of voice again. I didn't dare risk answering her. Pop went outside mumbling something about fixing the plough, and I envied him – he had every reason to get out of the house, being a man, but I was shut indoors on a battlefield of women's work with Mom. Everything I did she picked holes in: dusting, polishing, sweeping, even making beds wasn't done the way she liked and had to be done over. I swear she did it just to be awkward.

By the time Pop had got the truck, I was speechless. Mom

found a dozen things to hold me back. There was no satisfying the woman. And all my good intentions curled up like ashes around me.

I didn't breathe easy till we were on the road to town. Pop was burbling on about Harry Welch and some idea he had for the lower pasture. I didn't pay him any mind.

'Don't git riled at your Mom,' he said confidentially. 'She's having one of those women's times.'

How dare *he* even say those words? The idea of him being intimate with what he called 'women's times'!

Miss Courtland called in mid-afternoon when things were slack. She nodded at me, and made a beeline for Sam. She was after getting him to display some religious posters, food for the soul, she said, and being Miss Courtland, she took him over with the idea.

'Monica will help, won't you,' she said, and I found myself up a step-ladder tacking pictures to the wall, stuff like loaves and wine and a text: *He Gives Us All Our Needs*. She whirled away with lots more good works to do, and Sam shook his head.

'I don't know as liquor and religion mix, Monica,' he said. 'She your teacher?'

I sensed disapproval.

'Yes?' I bristled.

'A fine handsome woman. Reckon she just never met the right man. A woman needs work to do, and she got to find something to do without she's got a house and a man and kids to take care of. Church is as good a place as any, I guess.'

But then Doris came in, and Sam's face took on that humble-dog look he always had when his wife was around. Everyone in town said Doris wore the pants in that house, which was a strange notion for a woman like her, all powder and frocks and handbags. Doris approved the posters, said it was a good thing to be mindful of Our Saviour at all times, and did Sam have a half-hour to come and look at a sweet hat she'd just lost her heart to?

Sam had time, and left me to mind the cafe. There was nothing doing, so I leaned on the hatch and Blackfoot Pete gave me a cigarette. He claimed to be quarter Indian, and maybe he was. He'd come through What Cheer as a teenager passing the hat for an itinerant preacher, Reverend Josiah Willis, travelling in an old van with hell-fire and demons painted on the side. Pete had fallen for a What Cheer girl and the Reverend had gone on alone, giving the couple his fulsome blessing. Pete had gotten settled and married, working on a farm, when his young wife had died giving birth and the child died with her. Pete turned into a wild man, drinking and brawling and weeping in public. He'd lost his house and Sam had taken him on to wash dishes and sleep out the back. Sam had built him a one-room shack after a year, when Doris proclaimed it wasn't hygienic to have a grown man sleep in the kitchen. Pete set up a tent every year at the Farm Show, and told fortunes under the name Blackfoot Pete, and it stuck. He read all sorts from a strange pack of ancient Tarot cards, he read palms, and was amiable enough until it came to Religion. Then his face would mask over, and he'd say nothing. Or if he was drunk, he'd start an endless tirade about poisoning minds and taking children from their natural kin. It seems Reverend Josiah Willis had adopted him from folks too poor to raise him, and the holy years on the road had given him much to be bitter about. Besides, Pete was known to smoke more than tobacco, and at these times, he would rave about visions and monsters in the sky. He claimed he could read the inside of people, for all the show they put on.

I liked Pete, he was easy to talk to, and when he gave me a cigarette there was never a murmur of anything further, like with most guys. Already he'd saved me from a couple of tables of boys out for a good time, and full of horse-shit, appearing at my shoulder and enquiring with soft menace:

'Something bothering you boys?'

'What do you reckon to that schoolteacher?' he said, blowing smoke.

'She's a really good teacher, Pete. You'd like her.'

'She comes in here and I can see this blaze of colour round her, wowie! That lady has scarlet and gold burning off her like flames! Pheeeee–oo! That is one powerful lady. You want to smoke-smoke?'

'Hell, no thanks, Pete,' I said, waving away the long, hand-rolled number he held out, 'I don't need that stuff.'

'Lemme just fry an onion to kill the smell. Lady Doris, the dragon of Sam, I bet she has a nose like an anteater!'

The stuff he was smoking made him silent.

'So what have I got round me, Pete?'

He looked at me and giggled.

'You want to know? Course you do! Oh, what has Monica got around her? Let me think it through. Customers call you away!'

I took my break around seven, and sat in the kitchen while Pete hustled burgers on to a garnished plate. Then he sat opposite me, his eyes teasing.

'Give me your hand, Monica. Damn,' he said, looking into the palm, 'there's a lot here. We better fix a session and sort it out. I won't give you the marriage and babbies shit I turn out for most ladies. Come by the back Wednesday and I'll give you the works.'

Wednesday was when Miss Courtland had asked me to the Christian Awareness Group. I had this sneaky feeling I'd feel a lot more natural around Pete and all his mysterious trickery.

'OK,' I said.

6

I was torn on Wednesday between Pete and the prayer meeting, and wound up going to neither. I felt somehow that the Tarot wouldn't be the best way of preparing myself for staying with Miss Courtland.

'That's cool,' said Pete. 'Things happen when they're meant to.'

I couldn't bring myself to take on an hour of the Reverend Taylor Hadley. He came into school once a week and pontificated about growing minds, the Lure of Satan and the Divine Plan of the Man Upstairs. That was enough religion for me. I went to the library and embarrassed the hell out of Zip Singer by saying Hello to him. If he could, I would, and I was surprised by how fast the time went by.

After Sam's, I went to Miss Courtland's place and the first thing she did was tell me to call her Margaret. I found it a little weird at first, but soon got used to the idea – after all, it was not school. She made me cocoa, which was kind of disgusting to taste, but I drank it anyway, while she played me something classical on a record – Bach, she said. Then she showed me to her spare room, all white paint and polished wood.

'I've left you some books in case you can't sleep,' she said. 'I'll call you in time for breakfast. I usually have a bath in the morning, but I expect I'll be up well before you. Goodnight, Monica. God bless.'

She smiled at me in this lovely warm way, and closed the door behind her. I sat on the bed and looked at the books. *Northanger Abbey*, *Vanity Fair*, and *The Life of Christ*. I dipped into the first and second as I lay in bed. The words swelled and rolled and had me at the end of a page without knowing what I'd read. I got my own book. I was reading *The Body in the Bag*, someone had left it in Sam's, and it was one hell of a story. The cover showed two G.I. Joe chins in a swirl of smoke and a raven-haired, scarlet-lipped beauty under a distant lamp-post. I couldn't put it down until I found out who'd done it, and I was guessing until the last page.

'So, bud, behind your country doctor's practice, you've been doing a nice line in private embalming. Doctor Randolph, I arrest you in the name of the law!'

The silver-haired doctor's saintly face became a desperate mask of evil. He scrabbled in his pocket, and before Rick McShane could stop him, slipped a deadly capsule between his corpse-white lips.

'I take the secret to my grave, McShane,' he hissed, then fell at the detective's feet, his body racked by violent spasms.

Rick McShane looked at the rigid body, slid his gun into his shoulder-holster, set fire to a cigarette and dialled.

'Some you win, some you lose,' he muttered as the switchboard connected him with the Chief.

Even better, I learnt from the lurid cover that I could follow Rick McShane through some twenty further stories. It was time to sleep, so I turned out the light and lay awake for a while in the unfamiliar creakings of a strange house.

Miss Courtland – Margaret – woke me around eight. She had brought coffee for both of us, and sat in the chair by my bed.

'Did you do any reading?' she said.

'A bit,' I said.

'Would you like to borrow any of these?' she said.

'Oh, please,' I said, and she lent me all three. I had no intention of touching *The Life of Christ*, the idea of it embarrassed the hell out of me, but the other two would be OK.

'Well,' she said, 'I must get off to school. You students don't realise how much goes on behind the scenes! I'll see you tonight.'

I waited until I heard the front door shut before I got up. Margaret's bathroom was like the rest of her: bright and neat and somehow extravagant, with a wall of foreign-looking tiles and a noticeboard of postcards from all over the world. I read the back of one of them, a view of Jerusalem: 'His Peace and

Joy to you from the Holy City!' I tacked it back up, feeling like I'd been snooping.

Thursday was much the same, only I had two hours with Margaret between school and Sam's. She took me through Jane Austen, and gave me a vivid word-picture of the sedate life of a rector's daughter in a time when there were no trains and cars. 'Imagine the silence, Monica!' No TV, no movies, no records, no radio. No wonder they all talked a blue streak – there was nothing but conversation and piano-playing in their houses. And everybody had servants who knew their place, touched their forelocks even. It was another world. Also, it was my roots: by rights I should have been raised there.

All my notions of gentility got knocked for six in Sam's. It was non-stop beers and leering – word had got around that Sam had the dangedest gal working for him and I got the offer of half a dozen dates before ten o'clock.

'You OK, Monica?' said Pete through the hatch.

'I been asked out by every bum in this place. Something's going on.'

'Bimbo McMahon's got a book on you, dear,' he said. 'They're all laying money on who'll get the first date.'

'I guess that means good profits for Bimbo,' I said. Bimbo ran a lottery on everything that happened in What Cheer. When things were a little quiet, which was most of the time, he'd take odds on flies taking off from a table-top, and have everyone sweating and cheering like it was Kentucky Derby Day.

I told Sam I'd like to get off a little early since there was half a dozen yoyos competing about who'd walk me home. I slipped out the back and in five minutes I was on Margaret's porch. I could hear a wonderful sad piano tune and waited until the last chord before I knocked.

'You're early,' she said, pleased, 'I was just trying out some Chopin. I'd like to carry on for a while.'

I sat curled up in a chair by the fire and let the music wash over me till bedtime. I don't know what I read, but it was bliss.

After that, I made a habit of leaving Sam's early, and raced back to her, music, talk, laughter – she was my oasis. Some weeks later, she said:

'Well, I've been bombarding you with my taste. What sort of music do you like?' I thought a while. Music I heard on the radio I liked sometimes, but I hadn't taken much notice of who was playing. Scoot had played Dakota Staton; Billie Holiday Mom played sometimes, all *my man done me wrong*, curling into your body like sweet pain; Blackfoot Pete had a cassette player in the kitchen, and played some weird stuff, Janis Joplin was one I really liked. And then there was Carnival music.

'I guess – pop music,' I said, 'Janis Joplin. I haven't listened to much. Billie Holiday, Dakota Staton. Jazz.'

'Jazz!' she said, laughing ruefully. 'I was invited to "jam along" with a jazz group once, when I was at university. They didn't have a score, and with my classical training, I was lost. They'd nod to me and give me a note and I was supposed to improvise. Couldn't do it!'

She finished on a note of astonishment.

'Let me play you the piece I've been trying, I think I've got it now,' she said, and I sat bathed in the haunting minor melody. It touched something in me, the wordless harmony, it made me feel noble, tragic, tearful. Then Margaret sat opposite me, and put a log on the fire.

'Like it?'

'Yeah.'

'You haven't made it to the discussion group yet,' she said.

'No. I've been going to the library.' And playing pool. And listening to Blackfoot Pete, raving hypnotically over the grill. She gave a half-smile then nodded.

'I'm sure you will come, when you feel drawn to it. Now, I want to discuss something else with you: not to be bandied around the school.'

She fixed her eyes on mine.

'Of course not,' I said, feeling really gosh-darn privileged.

'Well, we've talked about college. What would you feel about going to England to study? Two years away from your family.'

My heart started racing. England! My real mother was in England, if she was still alive. Two years away from What Cheer, and Mom and Pop – it would be wonderful!

'Yeah. Sure. What do I do?'

'I thought you'd like it.' She smiled approvingly. 'I wrote to my old university and found that they have scholarship places for American students. I seem to recall Americans when I was there – we called them the gum-chewing fraternity. That's

England for you. *Any*way, I think you'd love it. It would give you a chance to really explore literature. It would be hard work, but I'm sure you could do it. Now you've started using the library, your essays are acquiring a maturity. I feel you're looking at things in depth. Your style is developing.'

I said nothing. My new blueprint for an essay was based on Zip Singer's success with Jane Austen. I'd tried out a few dry-as-dust phrases lifted from some of the dullest books ever been written. Stuff like 'the subtle use of metaphor underlines the delicacy of feeling between the principal characters'. Very *perceptive*, wrote Miss Margaret Courtland. I reckoned I'd throw in the words simile, metaphor, symbolism, ambivalent, at least once in an essay; then if I found a contemporary political topic and drew a parallel with the action of the story, I was home and dry. It did take some of the punch out of a book to strip it down that way. Like an autopsy. I could describe every bone and muscle, but it missed the breath and life of a walking, talking being. But it was clearly right for English essays, Miss Courtland was pleased, and what the hell.

I could still have a good time with Rick McShane, and I'd joined the *Crime Writers' Monthly* club. Right now, I was knocked for a loop by a guy called Raymond Chandler, and just itching to get the next month's selection.

'So,' said Margaret, 'what you would need to do is first ask your parents how they feel about losing you for two years.'

Uh-huh. Pop wouldn't even notice. It would give Mom no one to pick on, but at the weekend she'd been muttering about getting me off their hands. She'd start on Scoot, never knowing that he was about set to hit the road anyhow. She could occupy herself with Rosemarie and the baby, her favourite reproachful topic at present. The only thing I'd miss about this place was time spent with Margaret.

'I don't think they'd mind,' I said.

'Oh, Monica, don't be so hard-boiled!' said Margaret, with a knowing smile. 'They do love you. You'd have to sit an exam for the scholarship. I could coach you for that. You also have to write a five-thousand-word essay on what you would gain from studying in England. But I don't see that as a problem. I could go through it with you. And,' she looked away as if embarrassed, 'I know the tutors who'd be assessing your work. I think that might help. What do you say? You've got the ability. I just wonder about uprooting you! You're so American!'

'Well,' I said, 'I really would like to go to England.'

I told her about being adopted. She was intrigued.

'Why didn't you tell me before! That makes it even better for you. When did you find out?'

I told her about the wedding and Pop and Harry Welch.

'Your Pop should be horse-whipped,' she said, colouring up. 'What a way to find out! Don't you want to find out about your mother? Heavens, I could be your mother for all you know!'

I blushed. I'd had that very thought one night when she came and sat on my bed and patted my shoulder. She was talking Jesus at the time, and I was painfully aware that it was only words for me.

'You could go on a quest in England – oh, yes, you must go!' she decreed. 'It all fits in!'

'I don't know where to start,' I said.

'Get your birth certificate,' she said, 'from St Catherine's House, in London. Oh dear, Monica, I wish I'd known about this before – I could have helped you. You poor girl. I'm so sorry.'

Well, it was nice to get this warm sympathy. God, Margaret Courtland was one good woman. That night, she came to my room again, in her wrap, with her hair in a thick plait over one shoulder. She sat and talked a long time about London, and finally bent over and kissed me on my brow. I slept like a sanctified baby.

The one penalty clause with this scholarship at Nordgarten College, London, England, is it was half-sponsored by the Church of England. Zip was OK on that account – he'd played the organ for the past three years in church and got confirmed. I'd have to start showing a real interest in all that God business. I was one suspicious woman slouching along to that first religious discussion group on Wednesday after school. Miss Courtland and Reverend Taylor Hadley sat at the front, and I tried to catch her eye. But no, this was not the time or the place. The subject was the Eternal Love of Christ.

'You all know the *Jaw* of Our Blessed Saviour,' began the Reverend, 'He has spoken to each and evrah-one of y'all. He has drawn y'all to his forgivin' bosom with His Jaw, purraise the Lord!'

All the kids around me mumbled: *Yiz, Lawd, We Bless Yuh, Lawd*, and other such stuff that embarrassed me. I had this urge to laugh, picturing a bleached jawbone like the one me and Scoot had chased each other with when we found it in a field. Then Mom had said it was filthy with dead germs and trashed it.

'We all require to testify to the manifestations of His Jaw in our life, Alleluia!' shouted the Reverend, leaping to his feet, and flinging both fists into the air. 'For has He not blessed us with His Light, thank you, Jesus! Has He not touched us with His Spirit? Brothers and sisters in Christ, let us thank and bless Him!'

I sat dumbfounded as, one by one, every kid there stood and piped up about how Jesus had helped them. He was a helluva guy, influencing drivers' licences, classroom grades, family disharmony, lustful thoughts and everything else besides. This spontaneous testifying rippled along the rows and I counted down to when it would hit me and me with nothing to say.

Miss Courtland stood as the guy next to me finished splurting on about how the Jaw of the Risen Lord had kept his Mom and Pop from fighting. She spoke with her eyes closed, her voice hushing the holy silence to a thrill of stillness.

'There are those among us who are desperate to be touched by the living, breathing Spirit. Let us now pray that His Spirit moves over every heart in this room.'

We all sat silent, and I closed my eyes. I knew she'd said it to save me. That phrase: *My life flashed before me*, became a palpable thing, and I thought of every mean thing I'd ever done to Mom and all the hate I had for Pop and desperately cast around for a way for it all to change. The atmosphere was charged and I really truly wanted to feel the thing they'd all been talking about. Every kid in the room was a decent, OK kind of kid, the type I'd dismissed all my life. I couldn't get rid of the echoing sardonic one-liners Mom threw my way about church-going fools: the bleary wretchedness of my Pop: *a man got to live decent but there's no call to stand up in church and brag about it*. I felt a wave of anger sweep through me, I was seeing scarlet and it was some relief when Lily McMahon began tinkling a hymn tune out of the piano and everybody started singing. Lily played well – another kid I'd written off as a blonde mouse doing her best against the odds of her flamboyant father, Bimbo. Every kid in the room had always struck me as pathetic, teacher-pleasing and dull. I ducked out of the hall and marched to Sam's, head down. Only when I'd thrown on my chosen uniform did I feel normal again. I decided that the Spirit of God was trying to shame me into some kind of change and I was damned if I would change, and double-damned if I wouldn't.

The cafe was quiet that night. Miss Courtland and the Reverend didn't show, which was a relief to me. It was going to be tough enough to assimilate this new dimension into my late-night chat with Margaret. About ten o'clock, Sam shrugged and gave me and Blackfoot Pete the night off.

'I'm seeing you clear now, Monica,' said Pete, hanging up his overall. 'You want to stop by and hear about it?'

Anything to postpone the moment I had to face Margaret! I sauntered round the back.

'Take a seat,' said Pete majestically. His room was full of Navajo blankets, and weird posters of spacey landscapes, and he strolled around, lighting incense and smiling.

'What I see is good so let's have some good sounds,' he said. This was Louis Prima the King, said Blackfoot Pete with awe. What I heard was an inimitable bounce and humour with a gritty self-mocking vocal – it was 'Just a Gigolo,' and old Louis couldn't keep the giggle out of the plaintive words. For the first time that night I felt relaxed.

'You want to smoke-smoke?' said Pete, concocting a long cigarette with his illegal added factor. The old boys said Pete's only passion was Mary Jane, and he sure rolled and rubbed like a man in love.

'OK,' I said, feeling the tendrils of the damned curl around my heart.

'Now, Monica,' said Pete, exhaling in a smooth stream, 'I've been watching you to see you clear. I'm torn, torn, because I see a true indigo, a purple with the light behind it and that means learning. About ever-y-thing. And then I see green, this growing, thrusting power. And then you have a pure circle of white! Yeah! No bullshit gets through to you, Monica. And those are your colours: purple, green and white! Here – take it slow!'

He handed me the cigarette, and I took it like it would burn my fingertips with the fires of hell. I breathed deep and thought *purple, green, white*, like something familiar to cling to. One of his pictures was archetypal icebergs floating in a chill turquoise sea. It seemed like the most beautiful thing I'd ever seen, and I could feel the crisp snow beneath my feet, the sure sting of an arctic wind on my cheeks. I handed back the cigarette and lay back against the cushions.

'What about boyfriends, huh?'

Pete's question was luxuriously lazy. He wanted to know, not just get some kind of Pop-kick out of what I'd say.

'Pete, I don't have one. I don't want one. You've seen the guys round here. Jeee–z!' All at once I was aware of glorious blasphemy, and it felt good.

'Just promise me something,' said Pete, inhaling and leaning back against a rainbow-striped cushion. 'If ever you want to bust your cherry, just for the hell of it, knock on my door.'

I tensed up: men were full of guile, Mom had said. Pop had said how easy it was for a girl to lose her name. But then I felt easy: this was Pete, making an offer like *you want a cigarette*, and sprawled away from me like he didn't give a shit.

'OK,' I said.

'And I ain't throwing you out, Monica, but don't you have to get yourself to that lion lady's house sometime tonight? Come and smoke when you have a little more time.'

Pete waved, a little half-turn of the hand as I stumbled out into the night. Somehow I found my way to Margaret's house, and knocked on the door.

'You're late,' she said. 'Never mind. I think it's bedtime.'

Pheeeee–ooooo!

Wordless I went to bed, and when she sat beside me, I felt numb. I could only mumble when she said that the way of a Christian was hard, but when she smoothed my hair I felt electric sparks all over my scalp and it was hard to breathe. She drifted from the room and left me in blackness.

So, there I was, floating on clouds of amethyst warmth, crazy darts of neon chartreuse flying through the dark, and a white-hot sun shining in the midnight hour. I had this absurd urge to fling the windows wide and fly out over What Cheer, spiral higher and higher over the wormcast streets and up into the bright-starred sky. Then Margaret coughed behind the wall, and I shrank under the covers and slept.

7

I woke with one thing clear. I couldn't risk another smoke with Pete: the lazy jesting innuendo confused me and drew me more strongly than I wished to be drawn. I knew it was just curiosity, a distorted shadow of the clear flame I'd burnt for Joanne Lee Hunter. I'd been in love. But some days Pete would smile at me in this *I know you* way over the hotplate, and I wondered what it would be like to have him do it to me. For sure it was not what I wanted. Sue Ann had held on to her virginity until a ring was glued to the appropriate finger and then told me she'd let Ted *do it* and It wasn't anything to get excited about. Her biggest excitement was wondering was she pregnant or not every month. Rosemarie had tied herself to Billy Bob and a bundle of squalling girl-baby named for me. Already she looked old and tired and spoke with an edge in her voice, another baby on the way. I had no wish to blow my only chance of freedom. Jesus, if I did get the scholarship, imagine having to turn it down for a kid I didn't want!

When I was not struggling with Jesus at a meeting, or sitting entranced at Margaret's feet, I worked at home to hush up Mom, or at Sam's, to add to my savings. England or not, I should have the wherewithal to leave this State in six months. When Sam asked me to help out on the stall he set up at the Farm Show, I was delighted: the wage was double and I'd get free entry too. Besides which, I'd be away from home for an entire weekend except for sleeping. I had to do all the cooking, seeing as how Blackfoot Pete was plying his trade as fortune-teller and seer in his fake Cherokee tent.

'Can I get a little service round here?' It was a rasping command.

I looked up from the spitting hotplate ready to give lip right back to anyone fool enough to start ordering *me* around. Huh!

58

And I swear to God, there on the spot, onions and dogs and burgers spattering around me, heels dug into the ooze under the stall, I fell in love like I never even knew. My heart jitterbugged all the way down to my boots and back again, and if I hadn't already been scarlet from the heat, I would have blushed like a Maui sunset.

She was standing still with a swagger rippling and easy from her fine high cheekbones to the muscled line of her shoulders, and a sassy curl to the two scarlet lips snaked around a black cheroot. Her denim shirt was open at the neck, and her skin was tanned and taut under a scarlet bandanna. Her eyes were a burning brown, like copper and black grapes burnished into one. She shifted the cheroot to a corner of her mouth and spoke with a glint of gold.

'Burger and fries, honey. And crack me a coke. My damn horse seems set on making me eat a bushel full of dirt.'

'Yup,' I said, all dumb hick and hopeless passion.

And while I hustled with the fries, flipped the burger and grabbed the ice-cold can, she lit another cheroot from the smouldering butt, and scratched her jaw with the jewelled handle of a whip.

Her stetson was garnished with a rhinestoned hatband reading TROUBLE. Jesus Christ on a raft! *She* was the woman rider billed all over town as *Terrible Tess Trenchard From Tennessee – TROUBLE IS MY MIDDLE NAME!* The woman all the boys at Sam's had been chewing over for weeks.

'I can't see any woman whuppin' our boys!'

'No sirree, nor me. Dadblamed women – she's outta the county, anyways. Must be a bunch of pansy boys up in Tennessee.'

'Yip! Ain't no good old What Cheer boy gonna let hisself be showed up by a woman.'

'Women jest don't got the ass for rodeo-riding, pardon me, Monica!'

But none of them had seen Terrible Tess. I'd put ten bucks on her for the hell of it, and now I knew my instinct had been right. Somehow I passed her order over the counter and she took it from me in rawhide gauntlets, tossed me five bucks and told me to keep the change.

'Best of luck,' I said, trying to deepen my voice to match hers, 'I got money riding on you.'

'Is that right?' she said with a smile full of smoke.

'Yeah,' I said.

'Well, how's about having a drink with me afterwards? You can buy me one with the winnings.'

'I'd like that,' I said. 'I'll get off at six.'

'Meet me in the tent. If you like.'

She tipped her hat-brim to me, and sauntered into the crowd, her broad shoulders carving a space around her. If you like!

Sam appeared later, breathing beer all over me.

'Y'all been busy, Monica? I got a little tied up in the tent. Business.' He belched. 'You want to get off for an hour? I can handle the stall.'

I looked in the rodeo programme. Tess was riding at four.

'OK, Sam,' I said, 'I won't be long. I have to get off at six, remember?'

'Yup,' he said, 'Sure. Got yourself a date?'

'Sure,' I said, and peeled off gloves and apron.

'That's the girl,' he said.

I barged through to the front of the crowd, and watched a few overgrown bozos do their fancy tricks. Then the speaker crackled with a fanfare:

'LAYDEEEZ AND GEMMUN, IT IS MY PROUD PRIVILEGE TO PRESENT ONE OF THE FINEST RIDERS IN THE WEST. THIS LIDDLE GIRL HAS RODE HER WAY OUTTA TENNES-SEE AND INTO THE HEARTS OF ALL OF US. LAYDEEZ! GEMMUM! I GIVE YOU THE TERROR OF THE PLAINS – TERRIBLE TESS!!!!!'

Liddle girl! For all I was smitten, I knew Tess had not been a girl, liddle or otherwise, for a lot more years than I'd been alive. And I didn't care. The crowd shifted around me.

'It don't seem nat'ral.'

'A woman?'

'Evvah woman dreams about a stallion between they legs, boy, till they meet me, heh heh!'

Tess had changed into scarlet, and rode round the ring real slow, like an empress on a platinum-blonde palomino. Her gaze swept the crowd and I thought she almost smiled as she passed me. This was the part of the rodeo when the riders showed their paces. Tess nodded up at the control box, and the 'Tennessee Waltz' filled the ring. She moved as one with the horse in extravagant circles, both heads dipping as they turned. As the music throbbed to its end, she leapt to the ground and bowed to the horse, who bowed back, then she turned for the thunderous applause. Next she had a Wild West routine, firing blanks every which way, leaping to sit backwards, sideways, forwards, and finally she flung herself right under the horse and they galloped round the ring with her scarlet body frozen as if fixed in flight, clouded by dust, barely two feet from the ground and the blur of hooves. Even the unshaven 'stallion' next to me was batting his paws together, stamping his hind legs and yipping.

Then the 'Death March' started, and Tess made a whole mime of being holed up by bandits, ducking behind the horse's neck, firing wildly ahead, until there was a machine-gun thunder from the speakers. She twitched, writhed, and flung herself full length to the ground, gave a final shudder and lay still. The horse galloped on a way, then stopped and looked back. It wheeled and high-stepped back to her body, nudged her, looked up and shook its head. Then it picked up her pistol, and at a final shot from the speakers, collapsed beside her, and died with its nose on her neck.

The crowd went wild, and me more than most.

Tess stood up, slipped the reins into her hand and made a flamboyant bow. She flung herself into the saddle, and lay with her feet on the horse's rump, arms behind her head on its neck, and rode out of the ring.

'Well, there's one liddle lady we'll be asking back, laydeez and gemmun! What a performance! Now, the judges are taking a liddle time on deciding, so we all suggest you take yourselves a liddle refreshment! Thank you very much!'

I escaped back to the stall, edged Sam out of my way, and grilled and fried like you've never seen.

'Nothing like a date to put back the roses,' said Sam, 'Y'all look like you seen yourself a vision, Monica!'

'Gimme a hot dog, Monica, huh?' It was Bimbo MacMahon, who'd taken my ten bucks three weeks before. 'I believe you have some considerable winnings to take offa me, girl. Shee-it!

I'd a never thought a woman would do it. Take my hat off to ya, girl. Women's intuition, huh?'

So Tess *had* won! He had reason to smile. Few had backed this out-of-state woman, and the odds were long. I watched as he counted out 350 bucks and handed it to me.

'Jeeez!' said Sam. 'What you gonna do with that money, Monica?'

I smiled as I buried the roll deep in my back pocket. Tess had brought me so many more miles nearer to leaving all this behind and a whole lot else. I owed her more than a drink.

I left Sam wailing about clearing up and borrowed Tess's stroll to the beer tent. I stopped on the way and blew a few bills on a purple shirt I'd passed every day that week. It had a sheen like still water in the sun, and flowers picked out in gold thread over the shoulders. Add some fancy lilac satin piping, pearl buttons, and a comb dragged through my hair in the cracked mirror back of the stall, and I was some vision of radiance, pushing through the racket and sweat in the beer tent.

Of course Tess was surrounded. What did I expect – a candle-lit table for two? I kind of hesitated on the edge of her winning circle. What if she said to everyone, *have a drink*? I stiffened, ready to edge away. Then her eyes lit on me, and her tanned face split into a huge grin, gold tooth and all.

'Waaall, lookie here – it's the lady who made my luck today. Come here, honey, and kiss a winner!'

'Y'all left warpaint all over her, Tess!' some guy crowed, as I blushed my way in and out of an iron grip and somehow was sitting right beside her.

'Not the first, and not the last,' she drawled, her arm resting idly along the back of my chair. 'What'll you drink, honey? It's on me.'

'I'll get you a drink,' I said, 'with my winnings.'

'Damned if you do!' she said. 'Hey, Joe, get a bottle of bourbon, and a glass for my friend here – what's your name, honey?'

'Monica!' I yelled in the uproar.

'Russian, huh? Sonya. I like it.'

You can't correct an idol. Besides, I might be Sonya anyway, originally.

Tess grabbed the square bottle and trickled the smoky

tobacco-coloured liquid into a glass that had appeared in front of me as if by magic.

'Here's to you, kid,' she said, and tossed her shot down in one. So did I. It made me speechless with fire, but I was damned if I'd cough in front of her.

'Good–oh,' she said, wrinkling her lips together.

I carried on drinking in the cloud of dazzle that sparkled round her every movement. Turned out that Joe was her manager, as he tried to talk bookings and interviews until she roared at him:

'Don't I pay your goddam rent, boy? Gimme a bit of peace! Can't I have a drink with a friend in a little peace? God's sake, Joe!'

'There's no talking to you, Tess,' he said finally. 'But go easy. With the bourbon. And other things. Carmella said to keep an eye on you, dammit!'

'Carmella, Carmella, bullshit,' jeered Tess, swinging the half-empty bottle in his face. 'Fuck Carmella. Tess is gonna have herself some fun.'

Joe shook his head and melted back into the crowd.

'Now, my li'l Russian *émigré*, tell me all about it,' said Tess, sprawling towards me. 'No, no, lemme guess. Your family had ta git outta Russia – revolution, y'know. 'Smaybe your grammaw. Countess. Yup? Every damn Russian got royal blood. Shit! I had a fuckin ballerina once. I got a real feel for people. You're aristocracy, Sonya, I knew it. Down on hard times. Honey, when I saw you so proud and so free on that itty-bitty hamburger stall, I said, Tess, you and Sonya got a lot in common. Refinement. We ain't the common herd. Ain't I right?'

She swivelled her head and stared at me.

'Yeah,' she said, 'class. I got a fuckin nose for it. You wanna know if anyone, anyone, in the whole US of A – goddammit, the *world* – got class, just ask me to look 'em over. And, honey, you got class.'

I slugged a fresh shot of bourbon, winced, and nodded. The woman talked a lot of sense, it seemed to me. I caught sight of my gleaming cuff and grinned. I'd been recognised as not belonging in this miserable no-horse town of What Cheer. We got a fresh bottle.

'It's kinda close in here,' said Tess. 'You wanna walk some?'

I'd have done a *pas-de-deux* down a pirate plank if she'd asked me. It was a little strange to walk when my feet were at least a mile from my head, but Tess's arm on my shoulders steered me around the clumps of good old boys and out into the dark. Her other hand clinked a bottle and two glasses, and we sashayed in this blur past the tents and trailers.

'We'll set a while,' said Tess, plumping down on the ground. I slumped against her. The cork made an echoing plop in the silence, and she passed a glass my way.

'Well, Sonya, here we are,' she said.

I managed 'Yup.'

'Sonya,' she said. 'Do you feel it too? There's something about today. I mean, shit and scrrr–ew! I been down on my luck. Yeah, Lady Luck's been two-timing me. *Me!* Tess Trenchard! Then I meet you and half an hour later I got the world in my hands – Queen of the Rodeo! It ain't easy for an old broad. You wanna know how old I am, Sonya?'

'OK.'

'I oughtta be old enough to know better,' she said and cackled, 'Sonya, Sonya, I love that name!'

'Hey, Tess,' I said. It was bugging me.

'Shit! Tell me about it, honey,' she said, breaking matches against her boot sole.

'My name's Monica. But it might not be. Thing is . . .'

'If you don't know your own name! Who the hell do I think I am? My name ain't Tess. Only it goes with Terrible and Trouble and all that Tennessee shit. My real name's Melanie Trenchard. It's a real sissy name, ain't it? Me–la–neeeeeeeeeeeeeeeeeee! Sounds like a goddam disease. I got *ME–LA–NIE!* So how come you don't know your own name, Sonya?'

'I was adopted.'

'Jeez!' Tess jerked away from me. 'My sister had a kid adopted. She'd be fourteen now.'

We sat in silence for a while, Tess puffing away at her cheroot, me sipping bourbon as much as I dared. The silence grew. In the distance I could hear a faint hum. Dancing had started in the beer tent. I felt the heat and steel of Tess's arm around my shoulders.

'Getting kinda cold, ain't it?' she said, and pulled me closer.

Through the bourbon numbness I could feel my heart improvising its own rhythms. Tess's breath was on my cheek, and her hard fingers drew my face round to hers. Her lips brushed at mine, and her hand stroked my neck. She was – *licking me*? Her tongue came between my lips and I just let go, melting into the ground. This was the sin been haunting me for ever since I could remember and it was glorious, wonderful, and I didn't care, I didn't care.

Tess murmured into my neck.

'So, how old are you, Monica, Sonya, whoever the hell you are?'

'I'm seventeen,' I said. For just exactly what the hell reason had she stopped and raised herself on one elbow?

'Tell me it isn't true, honey!' she said.

'Yeah, I'm seventeen,' I said.

'Fuck it!' she said, 'I'm old enough to be your maiden aunt! Jeez! You never been with a woman before?'

'No,' I said.

'Aw, shit, honey. Y'see, I got this house rule. No screwing with under-age. Aw, shit.'

She lit a cheroot, and ruffled my hair. Which was a little like being given a bike when daddy's promised you a Chevy Malibu. My whole body was thrilling me like it never had before, and I didn't know what more there was, but I wanted more. I reached out and tried to pull her back.

'I'm fifty-three, Monica,' she said, 'I tried to kid myself you were twenty, twenty-five. Monica. *Seventeen!* I can't do it.'

I poured myself more bourbon.

'Aw, shee–it,' she said, lighting another cheroot, 'Y'see, I have this friend, Carmella. She kind of pulled me together when I really hit it. But she's like a sister. Oh sure, we live together. But like nuns, honey, else I'd never have started this foolishness. I tell you what. You get a bit older and come out and stay at the ranch. Carmella goes away sometimes. I got a ranch. Buena Vista. Yeah. You do that. I'll write you and let you know when. Gimme your address.'

I scribbled on a dollar bill and she folded it carefully and put it in her pocket.

'Honey, we better get back,' she said, rising and pulling me to my feet.

I stumbled along in her wake, and when we neared the tent, she let go of my hand and hugged me.

'It's been fun, Sonya, shit, Monica,' she said. 'We'll have some more fun, huh? Give yourself a little time, sugar.'

Back in the tent there were a thousand guys wanting to drink, dance and yabber-blabber with the Queen of the Rodeo. I dropped back as she became part of the crowd. My eyes lit on a familiar face, a short guy looking real cool.

'Scoot,' I said, clutching at his arm, 'would you escort your drunken sister home?'

'I'd be honoured,' he said, and we walked out of the place like Rhett Butler and Scarlett O'Hara.

My hands shook as I opened the letter postmarked Tennessee. I dashed off a note to Mom, and caught a ride. Twenty-four hours later found me travel-stained but light-hearted, taking long strides up a dirt road signposted 'La Buena Vista', prop. T. Trenchard.

Tess opened the door to me, and squashed the breath out of my body.

'You got here!' she said.

'Yup,' I said, and sprawled in a leather chair while she threw a cocktail together.

'Monica, you aiming to raise yourself outta that bed? You got five minutes till the school bus!'

I could smell acres of clover and a sharp mountain-tinted freshness in the air when I woke. I sat up against the satin pillows, and Tess waltzed in, in a silk kimono the colour of pomegranates.

'I brought you coffee, Monica,' she said. 'I'd like to start each day with you.'

She poured steaming coffee into an eggshell-thin cup. I flung back the sheets, and said 'Come to Momma!' She slid in beside me.

'Of course, the theory of relativity is one with which Miss Robinson feels so familiar that she can pay it no attention! Monica, what did I just say?'

I woke up on the second morning at 'La Buena Vista', turned over, and wrapped myself round the smooth curve of Tess's back. She gripped my hand, then turned over and we melted into each other from head to toe.

'Monica! Would you do me the courtesy of answering the question?'

'Yes, Miss Courtland,' I said, feeling embarrassed. For goodness' sake! I couldn't even concentrate in English these days and me with a scholarship hope the pride and joy of the whole school. I felt really guilty after all Margaret had done for me, but to tell the truth I was finding it difficult to fake an interest in anything since the Rodeo. Since Tess.

8

I felt very distant from everything at home. Mom was still blitzing every room in the house, and I found myself chores that kept me separate from her. Sometimes she would say awkwardly:

'I think we've done enough, Monica. You want some coffee?'

I would take my coffee up to my room and get on with schoolwork, leaving her sitting alone and pinched at the kitchen table. I had four months to the scholarship and the thought that I might fail terrified me. In my mind I was already at the Nordgarten College, retracing Margaret's hallowed steps. I marked the days off on the calendar.

I found myself tolerating Pop more than I ever had done before. So he was a drunk – at least you could rely on his moods and he let me be. I'd never been frightened of him. These days he seemed old and pathetic. He'd made nothing of his life. Mealtimes he would blabber something about me seeing the sights of Europe and under Mom's glare I would go along with it. One evening he took me upstairs to the attic and hauled out an old tea-chest.

'My souvenirs, hon,' he said. 'Tell you what, you git this scholarship and you can have my Air Force kitbag. Always thought I'd be givin' it to the boy, but he'll never get hisself a commission. Danged if I know what he will do. I'll never make it back to Europe, but this here bag can do a little travelling on my account.'

Last thing at night, I found the kitbag on my bed.

'I haven't got the scholarship yet, Pop,' I said to him the next morning. He just grinned and swore up and down there was no 'if' about it. Mom hushed any such talk; it was bad luck to count your chickens, and daydreaming fools came to no good. There's no way on earth I'd ever have thought of me and Pop as friends, but now that we'd both been through the acid bath of Mom's scorn, we had something in common. Mom talked in this weary way from time to time about just suppose I did get through, then we'd have to get me some new outfits and a decent case, but I kind of liked the idea of Pop's kitbag and as for new outfits – jeans suited me fine.

I was just marking time until leaving, and only felt truly alive when I was with Miss Courtland – Margaret. She was so kind to me. We'd spend long hours after Sam's had closed talking about England and music and books. I'd been going to the religious meetings, well, religiously. I wanted to feel this Spirit of Christ they talked about with lit faces. I felt like an outsider when they got going. God knows I wanted to sincerely say *I believe, Lord!* But I couldn't. Their ecstasy I could only match with my earthly experiences of Joanne Lee Hunter and Tess. I was coming to the conclusion that I was one of the damned, and only being alone with Margaret took me anywhere near the Joy they talked of with such sincerity.

She told me she prayed for me, and followed this up with late-night talks when I was in bed. Then I almost felt holy. But away from her there were so many things luring me to what Reverend Taylor Hadley called Sin. Blackfoot Pete kept up his gentle, insistent line of worldly delights; Scoot confided that there was nothing like a widder woman to make you feel alive; the one thing Mom and Pop agreed on was that Jesus was not to be found on this earth, and religious folk were a sanctified bunch of Bible-spouting, self-deluding jackasses. I didn't bother arguing with them: that would have let Mom know I cared and given her ammunition to mock me with.

One week, Margaret told me a healer was coming to What Cheer. She showed me the leaflet, with a picture of Preacher John Dettweiler and his wife smiling out at you, like an election poster over a caption:

This leaflet may change YOUR Life!
Do you dare read on?

I looked at Margaret and she smiled, like a quiet challenge.

Over the years, my wife Lucy and I have come to know Jesus as our Personal Saviour. I started life as a salesman and was making a good income for our family. We had our own house, three lovely children, and Lucy was even able to run her own small business at home when the children went to school. *We had everything!*

But still we wanted more, and money worries began to plague us and come between us. We started having rows, even in front of the kids. Then one day, at a conference of salesmen, I met a man like me, successful, married, and I took to him straight away. I'll call him Samuel for the Word of the Lord was surely with *him*.

Samuel had something I envied: a Joy and Inner Peace I'd never come across before. In the evenings I noticed that Samuel was never in the bar drinking and talking sales figures with the rest of us and I asked him about it. He looked me straight in the eye and said: *I've found Jesus.* That evening he gave me a treasure greater than any of the material goods I'd so carefully hoarded – he gave me a Bible.

As I read the Blessed Word in that motel room in Milwaukee, I found myself moved to tears. *This* was what my Life had been missing: *this* was what gave Samuel his Inner Peace, and I fell on my knees and prayed for forgiveness for the empty life I'd been leading. Samuel came by and prayed with me, and the next day I went home.

I was terrified driving back: what would I say to my wife? I knew that Jesus would give me the words, and that this new Truth mattered more than anything else in Life. Well, Praise the Lord! Lucy listened to what I said and Jesus touched her heart. That evening we prayed together for the first time and committed our lives to His service. As soon as we could, we joined our local Church and began to live in our Community as Christians.

It was some years later that the Lord spoke to me direct:
'Give up your job for Me, John.'

'You know what you're doing, Lord,' I said. He had given me every reason to trust to His Goodness. With Lucy at my side, I threw in everything I'd known as security, and since that day He has showered me with an abundance of His gifts. To think I was worried about giving up a salary and a profession! I've never had an idle moment since I put myself in His loving hands, Alleluia! His Spirit is in me when I am among the lost and lonely, and when I touch those weary brows, and unhappy shoulders, I can feel His Loving Power move through me in the Gift of Healing!

Brothers and Sisters in Christ, I implore you to bring your burdens to His Loving Feet. He has made the lame walk and the blind see and I have witnessed this with my own eyes! PRAISE HIM!

Stirring stuff! I had wanted to feel this Spirit ever since that first meeting when I'd sat dumb as a dope on the outside of it all.

'Will you come?' said Margaret, the most serious I'd ever known her. When I nodded, she came over and knelt beside me and took both my hands in hers.

'I know your path is hard at the moment,' she said, 'but He has a plan for you and it will all work out in time. It's your birthright.'

Moments later she was the teacher again, paring down my latest essay, goading me to be precise, to abandon some of the best lines I'd written, saying there was no need to be flip. I nodded dumbly, my hands glowing where she had held them so tight.

Mom took my announcement in silence, raising an eyebrow over the pan of greens.

'I guess you have to find out for yourself,' she said finally. She had grown very quiet with me of late; she acted hurt whenever I went to stay with Margaret, but I took that with a pinch of salt. I was doing my share round the house, wasn't I? And she could hardly be missing my company: any time I spent with her was wordless and uneasy these days. We only ever talked when I told her the times I'd be out and away with Margaret. That and plugging away at the scholarship assignments were all I did outside of school and Sam's. But I had learnt to time what I told her. The week before the healer was due, for example, Margaret had asked me to spend the Sunday with her visiting an outlying farm, with religious books. I'd be spending Saturday night at her place – telling Mom could wait till the Friday before.

And this time she was really hurt and lashed out at me. Rosemarie and Billy Bob and my little namesake were coming over for the Sunday.

'Surely to goodness you could afford a little time with your own family, Monica?' she said sharply. 'We don't hardly see you these days. Seems to me you might be overstaying your welcome with this Miss Courtland – your precious Margaret. In my day there wasn't none of this first-name business. Oh, I know, you've told me often enough, she's grooming you for this scholarship. But Sunday is a day of rest, ain't it? Or has that changed with the rest of it?'

'Leave her be, Kathereen,' said Pop. 'She's gonna make something of herself, and we can't hold her back.'

'Hush your foolish tongue,' said Mom angrily. 'What about honour thy father and mother? One of them holy commandments I don't see you respecting, madam.'

In my head I said *But you aren't my mother and father*. That was a thought that came to me often these days. Margaret and I had talked a lot about my real mother, and she'd made me feel better about the total indifference I had towards Willard and Katherine Robinson. She said that even natural kin you don't always get on with, and there's even less reason to get on with people that don't have your blood. The idea pleased me, although at first I felt like I was betraying them. But Margaret had said it and soon it was gospel to me along with everything else.

Sunday morning Margaret woke me after she'd been to church. We were going together later in the evening. I bathed and dressed and joined her downstairs. She had a big box of books ready to take and a picnic hamper for us to share in the afternoon. We drank coffee, ate toast and honey and were in her car before most folks were stirring. The farm we were headed for was a couple of hours away and by the time we got there we were both singing gospel tunes and laughing in the bright new day. I followed her across the yard with the books and she winked as she knocked on the peeling door. A chorus of barking started and a small raggy child opened the door barefoot. When he saw it was Margaret he grinned and hollered:

'Pop, it's that lady!'

His Pop appeared, a grey-faced, unshaven man, children trailing at his heels, a tear-stained infant in his arms.

'Miz Courtland, what a blessin' t'see yuh. Mary Lou been on

at me to git the house straight, bein' as she cain't raise herself, but I had the baby up half the night with bellyache and . . .'

'You don't have to clear up for me!' said Margaret. 'I didn't come to see a tidy house, I came to see all of you. This is my friend Monica. Monica, this is Jim Smallbone and Andy, Ruth, Joshua and little Rachel.'

The kids stared at me the way kids do, and Jim said it was a pleasure t'meet any friend of Miz Courtland.

'I'll go and see Mary Lou,' said Margaret and whisked away, with Jim trailing behind her apologising for the state of the place. I went into the kitchen, feeling kind of redundant. I'd been prepared for prayers in the parlour and a little chat. I'd never seen such squalor in my life. The kids had clearly been left to their own ideas about breakfast, and the table was awash with trails of milk, soggy handfuls of cereal, and jelly-smeared crusts. The sink was piled with every dish in creation; a half-dozen mangy kittens were fighting in the dust and grit on the floor, and every surface was littered with boxes and half-empty jars. The kids stared at me like a pack of wild dogs.

'Howsabout if we clear this up, huh?' I said to Andy.

'Not me, sister,' he said, 'I'm a boy! And the others is too small. Miz Courtland generally fixes the place up.'

They scat out into the yard whooping and screeching. So Margaret generally did this, did she? At least I could make myself useful. But where the hell to begin? I found a filthy plastic garbage bin and piled the trash into it. There wasn't a cloth in the place, so I ripped up a ragged dishtowel and scalded the table as clean as it would go and wiped the surfaces. The tap-water was rusty and cold, but I filled a pan and lit the gas under it to wash up. The dirty dishes I piled away from the sink, gagging at the stench of mould. I scrubbed the sink with a bald brush before I could wash anything in it; I slooshed floods of soapy water over the draining board before I could put a dish there to dry. And then there was the floor. I smiled wryly at the notion Mom had of me being a gracious lady as I scraped the worst debris from the tiles, and scrubbed away on my knees. I even had to wash the clotted filth from the handle of the kettle before I could set it on the gas. This place was disgusting, and I set to on the grease-streaked cupboard doors as the kettle boiled.

73

Andy and Ruth and Joshua and Rachel came barnstorming muck all over the floor before I could stop them.

'You kids got shoes?'

'Nope,' said Andy, dabbling grey-brown toes across the damp floor.

'Well, I'll tell you what,' I said, 'I'm going to put a pan of water on the back step, and a towel, and you get your feet clean and dry before you come in here.'

I sounded like Mom.

'You ain't like Miz Courtland. She gives us cookies,' said Andy.

'Yeah,' said Rachel in this gruff little voice.

'Oh yeah?' I said. 'Well, maybe I'll give you cookies. Get your feet washed and we'll see.'

Andy stared at me and squared his shoulders. He led the four out in Indian file to the chant of *we don't like Monica, we hate Monica*. I can't say my heart was broken to hear it. God, if I had kids! The kettle was taking an age to boil, Margaret was taking an age upstairs and I looked around the transformed kitchen. To hell with it! I sat on the back step and lit a cigarette. The kids stared balefully at me from the fence. *Oh, what a beautiful morning!*

Jim stepped over me, my-my-ing about what a woman's touch could do in the home. It took him all of two sentences to ask me for a cigarette, and we sat smoking while the baby crawled red dirt all over the clean clothes he'd put her in.

'Miz Courtland is a blessin' to us,' he said. 'Yessir. Mary Lou always been a religious woman and since she's been took bad she's had two worries – the kids, and not gittin' in to church. I do what I can, but a man ain't made for raisin' kids. And I ain't much for book-larnin', cain't even read the Good Book beyond what I know. Miz Courtland's our reg'lar little angel. Dammee, who's put that pan on the step?'

'I did,' I said. 'I told the kids they could wash their feet before they come in and muck up the floor.'

'Damned, excuse me, I'll be ding-blasted if you don't recall my own mother, God rest her soul. She'd always have us kids under the tap at th'end of the day afore we wuz allowed indoors. Y'all gonna make a fine wife one of these days.'

The thought of a string of grimy brats and a no-hope tenant

74

farm! I wished Margaret would hurry up. When she did come down she exclaimed over the kitchen and called the kids in.

'*She* says we gotta wash our feet afore we git in,' said Andy.

Margaret only laughed and made a game of it. Andy stared at me triumphantly as she dried his feet. Then she lined them up at the table and asked them their commandments. They chanted the answers and every one they got right, she gave them a cookie. It took for ever.

Jim said wouldn't we stay for a bite. My heart sank, then Margaret looked at her watch, exclaimed at the time and said we had a lot more to do. Her shoulders were shaking as we drove out of the gate and she let out a huge laugh a little way down the road.

'Monica,' she said, 'you are priceless! I've never seen Andy's face so set: and you standing there like the avenging Angel! Wash their feet! You looked just how your mother sounds! Bless you for ploughing through the filth. I'm sorry I had to leave you so long.'

I relaxed in the warmth of her smile.

'Where are we going?'

'Wait and see!'

She took a dirt track off the highway and the road got bumpier and rougher as we climbed the twists and turns, past fields of astonished cattle, broken sheds and dry trees. We rounded a hairpin bend and she stopped the car on a patch of grass where the track ended.

'Look!' she said, one wave of her arm giving me the whole vista. In the distance I could see a flat, low-winding river, and farms like toy houses here and there. The sun was blazing from a perfect blue sky, and we walked to the edge of the hilltop.

'I love it here,' she said, jerking her hair free with one movement. 'Feel the wind!'

I marvelled at the sunlight edging her face, and the wind lifting her hair as she stood, eyes closed. Goddam it! I wanted to hold her hand. I steeled myself against the unworthy thought and pushed down the surge of wild feelings that pulsed through my body. Tess had been only a pale shadow of this! Now I knew I was damned: even here, even with Margaret, the unholy desires were a part of me.

She didn't notice, just turned and smiled at me, then strode over to the car and swept the picnic basket on to the grass. Eating in our house was what you did to feed yourself and create work and trouble for Mom. The idea that you should relish a meal! Margaret laid out the food with gusto, announcing each foil-wrapped delicacy like a queen at a banquet. It was infectious, and I savoured everything there, amazed that there was so much joy and happiness to be had in the world. Then Margaret lay back on the ground and closed her eyes. Oh, Jesus! I wished she hadn't done that. I'd been able to squash the urge to touch her by not looking at her direct, but how could I not look at her, spread out in front of me, glorious, unattainable . . .

'Penny for your thoughts?' she said.

'Nothing,' I said, blushing crimson. I lay down too. It seemed the safest thing.

'This has always been my place,' she said softly. 'Now it's ours. It's the most beautiful place I've found out here. Homesick for the hills and a bit of green. You probably already know it. Do you?'

'No,' I said, concentrating on an insect dragging a bit of twig by my head. Every word she said thrilled me right through.

I dozed off and woke to her laughing face; she was tickling me with a piece of grass. The sun was lower now, and the golden light moulded her cheekbones and splashed along her lips. Her cheeks were soft rose. We busied ourselves packing up, and I didn't let myself meet her eyes. I wasn't about to make a total fool of myself.

'Let's say goodbye to this place – make it *au revoir*,' she said. 'We'll be back.'

I followed her to the edge and stood awkwardly at her side while she breathed deep. I wanted to let go and say all the things beating on my tongue, but that way would lead to banishment, I was sure. Courtly damn love, again. *Though I am nothing to her, though she may rarely look at me, and though I may never woo her – I'll love her till I die.* The noble words played through my mind and I made my pledge in silence. We went back to the car. She eased it down the darkening track, freewheeling.

'You're very quiet,' she said. I nodded like a fool.

What the hell? Her hand came away from the steering wheel

and she clasped mine like it was the most natural thing in the world. I gripped the strong warmth, like I was drowning and her hand was a spar in the ocean. Half-way down the track, she put on the handbrake and turned to face me. I was full of dread. Had she divined my thoughts?

'There's something we've forgotten,' she said, squeezed my hand and let go. She reached behind and pulled a bottle from the picnic basket.

'I got us some wine,' she said, and poured it out and gave me mine. 'Here's to your thoughts! You've been bursting with them all afternoon – tell me!'

We touched glasses and the pure sound rang through the silence. What was I to say? I wished to hell I wasn't me, I wished I didn't have these thoughts, I wished I could come up with something high-minded – anything but the truth! I gulped the wine and the heat rushed around in my chest. She took the glass from me.

'You're very troubled,' she said wonderingly, and drew me close to her. 'What is it?'

All I could do was cry like a baby as she rocked me close in her arms, her wonderful, loving arms.

9

Somehow she drove home still holding my hand, and any time she let go, she gave me a little squeeze, like *I'll be back*. I didn't trust myself to speak, words might have burst this incredible shimmering bubble of happiness.

Back in What Cheer, I felt calm and whole, my life fallen into place. In church I said all the responses and, for the first time, I meant every word. Joy? I was cocooned in it. Love? It filled my heart like a sheet of flame. Peace? I was floating on an ocean of peace. And *she* was by my side with her radiant face. I knew she felt it too.

And there was still a whole evening with her, before it would be Monday.

'Did you enjoy today?' she asked me as we ate supper. I looked her straight in the eye and said yes.

She talked on about Jim Smallbone and Mary Lou and the children. I was fixed on the way her mouth moved and wanted to lean over and stroke her lips with my finger. I could have died and gone to heaven that moment.

'John Dettweiler and Lucy will be here on Tuesday,' she said, 'For the healing meeting. I met them in Washington a few years ago. They're staying here.'

I went cold: did this mean I couldn't?

'You'll like them,' she went on, and I started to breathe again. Then she pulled out the Scrabble board. We had two versions of this: an American and an English one. I always won American, when you could put down ordinary words that she called slang. And the hours ticked by to bedtime. I knew where I wanted to sleep: by her side, in her arms, and my mind clouded into overdrive beyond that. We went upstairs together, then she turned at her door and hugged me.

'Good night, Monica,' she said. 'Thank you for today.'

And closed the door. I tiptoed to my room in shock. Was I meant to knock? Didn't she want me there? I couldn't have put into words what I was feeling. I settled myself in bed and waited for her to come to me. She didn't. Was this playing hard to get? I didn't like to think of her, of *us*, doing any such foolish thing. This love was sacred, pure and holy. I could wait till she was ready, and composed myself for sleep.

There was no question in my mind about what was going on. For some absurd reason, Lady Luck had finally lit on me, and through Monday and Tuesday I played out all the corny phrases from every romance and love song I'd ever read or heard . . .

You are everything, and everything is you . . . If you were the only girl in the world . . . You are the sunshine of my life. Sometimes even I dared to think: *and then I kissed her . . . Take me in your arms and rock me, baby!* The idea gave me a tantalising sensation all through my body. I strolled around the place like I'd won a million bucks, I could afford to be nice to Mom – I had the secret of life in the palm of my hand, *the love of a good woman!* Was there ever love like this before? I found myself smiling at all sorts of things, at nothing at all, the world suddenly seemed three-dimensional and beautiful and it was all mine. And I was more than nice to Mom, I felt tender and sad at the worry lines scored over her face, her petty nagging, the dismal round of duty that she had made of her life.

The one thing on my mind was how we'd cope with me being away for two years. I could handle it if she could, and after all, she might come to England to see me if it all got too much. I went to her house on Tuesday after school, and a strange man opened the door.

'John Dettweiler, praise the Lord!' he said, with the same cheesecake smile I'd seen on the leaflet. He clasped my hand and drew me into the living-room. His wife Lucy sat there deep in conversation with Margaret, who acknowledged me with a brief smile. Lucy struck me as a silly woman, Landsaking and Gracious goodnessing away and I wondered that Margaret could listen so intently, like she really was interested. I sat with an ear on Preacher John, revealing in the wonderful stillness, the majesty of the one I loved.

Preacher John talked like his pamphlet, the flaming Sword of the Lord, he said, cleaved to his hand as he worked on towards the Promised Land. He told me Margaret had a mighty high opinion of me, and I glowed. Him and Lucy always fasted before a big meeting, he went on, so we were all going over to Sam's for what he called an Ágape feast afterwards. Ágape meant love, he said, and I nodded. How right it all was! Margaret drove us along to the crowded hall, and I sat up front beside her, loving the way her strong hands moved the wheel. She smiled at me when she parked the car.

'I'm so glad you're here!' she said. I smiled back, no, I grinned back, my face was having to stretch into an openness I'd never known before I knew her this way.

We went and sat in the front row. Just about everybody in the county had come down to What Cheer for this meeting. There were hymns and prayers and testifying, and Margaret nudged me to go up and speak. But I couldn't – all I had to say was private between her and me. So up she went and I gazed at her beautiful face and drank in every word.

She said she'd been a stranger in a strange land, brought here by the Love of God. She said she'd found it all new and different at first, been put off by the dry earth and the newness of our tight-mouthed landscape. And then she'd found a new Joy in her work, and all sorts of unexpected people to share it with. I knew she meant me. I felt like a cream-fed kitten. When she sat next to me, I knew my face was as lit up as hers, and we all prayed together.

Then the healing part began, and people filed out of their chairs to line up in front of Preacher John and Lucy. What did I need with healing, I thought, with the purity of belonging and loving a white-hot reality inside me? But then I thought of Margaret's closed door and the uneasy dread I'd felt – maybe a little healing would clear away all my doubts. I lined up with the rest.

The queue of people split at the rostrum, and you went either to Preacher John or to Lucy, depending on who was free. I didn't want to go to Lucy, but had this kind of dread that I would. Behind each weeping person being healed were a couple of big guys who caught those who passed out in the Spirit of the Lord. Zapped by Jesus, the way Preacher John had said. I didn't want to do that either, as I saw them lift the limp bodies to the nearest chair.

Sure enough, I got Lucy. She looked like Nancy Reagan, from her good-little-wife permanent to her sensible suit and floppy-bowed shirt. She fluttered one hand over to my brow as I stood there.

'We purrr–ay for our sufferin' sister,' she whispered, 'Oh, Lord, yes we do indeed! You know what is troubling her in her heart, and I ask You, in the name of Your Son, Our Blessed Saviour, to reach in, reach in, with Your kindness and hope.'

She finished on a wailing bleat and gave me a huge shove with her palm. I staggered and the big guys flanking me caught me and led me to a chair. Out in the Spirit? More like thrown off guard and not expecting old Lucy's ladylike arms to have the kick of a mule. What a charlatan! I found my way back to Margaret, smarting with the feeling of being cheated. But she wasn't there: she was in front of Preacher John, whose voice rose in a strange chanting as he made signs over her. Maybe he was the real thing, I thought, and closed my eyes as Margaret returned.

I sure was a spare part while we drove back to Sam's. Lucy was twittering on about How Great is Thy Love, Lord, and wasn't it a lovely meeting, just like she'd cleaned up at a rummage sale. Preacher John was puffing and blowing with self-satisfaction. Margaret was humming a strange tune and smiling abstractedly. *Jesus!* I thought, and waited for the lightning bolt to strike me down. It didn't.

Sam's was humming, and we had to wait for a table. Blackfoot Pete beckoned me over.

'You want to give me the order? Save you and your holy friends a bit of time. How'd it go?' His knowing Cherokee eyes twinkled at me and he made an absurd face in the direction of Margaret, Lucy and old John-boy. I shrugged.

When we all sat, Preacher John made a loud blessing over the table. I could have died of shame. But Christians are always persecuted for their beliefs. He followed up by ordering *the fruits of the vine*, and booming on about how great it was to share a meal in Love.

'I'll bring ours over,' I said to Sam, who was bumbling about in a vague, harassed way. Pete set our plates on the hatch with a flourish. He'd gone to town on the salad.

'Holy onion rings!' he hissed, 'I got inspired seeing all those cock-eyed haloes floating over you people.'

'Screw you, Pete,' I said. I wouldn't have Margaret and me lumped in with these two fakers.

'So you're Margaret's little protégée?' said Lucy, dicing her food into bite-sized strata: a little meat, a little salad, a skewered french fry. Protégée? I looked at Margaret, and she gave me a reassuring smile.

'I guess,' I said.

'Like a bloom in the desert,' said Preacher John, lyrically, beating ketchup out of the bottle in globs. 'I said to Margaret, that's dry country you're going to down there. Twisty plants that look dead with a core of sap deep inside. A sun that heats you and burns you up. But His Love produces wells and springs and floods from barren rock, doesn't it?'

I was trying to figure out if I was the sap, the twisty plant, the rock, the spring, or what, when Margaret spoke.

'Monica's kept me sane the past few years,' she said, catching my eye, 'haven't you? The standards at the school aren't quite what I'm used to.'

'Intellectual arrogance,' intoned Preacher John, wiping his lips. 'And I thought we'd knocked that out of you in Washington!'

I didn't like that. Still less the patronising way he covered Margaret's hand with his. She only smiled and patted his arm. God, she was some tolerant woman!

'Well, I think all that's been put to rights,' she said. 'Monica and another boy are the only ones capable of university standards, but I think everyone enjoys books a little more since I've been here? And there's the religious discussion group. That's been most productive.'

'Yes,' I said. 'You've got everyone thinking.'

Margaret looked pleased and Preacher John well-welled and said it was praise indeed, like I'd been real cute or something. Suddenly a familiar voice howled him down: Janis Joplin wired up to all four speakers at full blast. Blackfoot Pete was having a good time, and appeared behind the bar, miming ecstasy to 'Piece of my Heart'.

Sam snapped off the power and apologised into the temporary darkness. I felt breath on my ear and Pete's wicked whisper:

'Having fun?'

The lights came on and he strolled nonchalantly round the back. I was crimson.

'What was that? Heavens, don't you think rock music is like all the devils in hell?' said Lucy. 'All that wailing and screaming?'

'Ask Monica – she likes pop music,' said Margaret, with a sly grin.

'That was Janis Joplin. Who killed herself with heroin and heartache,' I said from Blackfoot Pete's lyrical biography of the woman he called the greatest white blues singer. They all tut-tutted.

'I hope you've never tampered with narcotics, Monica,' said Lucy.

'No,' I said. I didn't count what I smoked with Blackfoot Pete. That was fun, a daydreaming time-killer racing me through the hours between Margaret and Margaret. It made me much better around Mom, too.

Back at Margaret's, Lucy got herself on the piano keyboard and we belted out some revival songs fit to wake the dead. Then she stretched archly, yawned and said:

'Gee, daddy, I'm all done in. Your little girl had better go and find herself some beauty sleep!'

Well, instead of throwing up on the floor, Preacher John smiled at her and said:

'You toddle up, sweetheart, and close your pretty eyes.'

'It is late, isn't it?' said Margaret. I rose to go as she added, 'I think John and I have a little more to do.'

'Lord bless you!' tinkled Lucy and I found myself going upstairs with her chittering nineteen to the dozen about the *charming* wallpaper, the *darling* carpet, the exquisite touch Margaret had at making a home, and wasn't it a shame the Lord hadn't led her to her chosen beloved like He'd done for her and John. She put a finger on her lips and asked me in a whisper *Was there anyone? Margaret was so secretive about these things!* It was to my credit that I played gosh-darned dumb gee-I-don't-know, Miz Dettweiler. I'd have loved to say that *I* was in love with Margaret, just to see her face. Lucy was a woman who flittered for hours going to bed, into the bathroom, swishing back to her room for face cream, *I'm such a little dreamer!* as she passed me in her floral wrap, and *I'm mortified being such a dither and a nuisance!* Finally she was through and I splashed my face and got to bed. Through the floor I could hear the sonorous tones of Preacher John and Margaret laughing back. Then they started singing, not so I could make out the words, to a tune I'd never heard before. It had a ringing harmony and then there was silence and more low voices in the darkness. I lay awake, sort of waiting for Margaret, but the minutes and hours went by with no sign of her, and finally I slept.

Morning came with Preacher John singing in the tub, and Lucy in a different flowered wrap sitting in the kitchen and taking all Margaret's time till school. I went and dressed after she had gone.

'Well, so long,' I said at the kitchen door.

'Bless you, Monica,' said Lucy, hugging me and kissing me with powdery lips. 'You take care of Margaret – you need each other. Come up and stay with us any time. God bless!'

I had to endure a barrel-chested embrace from Preacher John and sloped off into the new day. This evening they'd be gone and I'd have her all to myself.

Pete was sardonic in the cafe that evening. He told me he could see tongues of flame licking around my no-bullshit halo of white light. I thwatted him with the nearest towel. He knew nothing! Besides, next week was the scholarship exam – I'd begged two evenings off before and after, nominally to prepare and recover. The truth was I'd do anything for more time with Margaret. She came in with Reverend Taylor Hadley later. They were deep in conversation and my heart lurched every time she clutched his arm. But I wasn't bothered – I knew her better now, and knew that when it was my time, she'd be all for me. God, it made me love her more, that gift she had for focusing in on whoever she was with. How we all needed her! And how she gave herself to us! And I knew my time with her was special to both of us. I could wait.

When I tore back to her place, she opened the door with a distracted expression. She shook it off after a moment, and we sat round the fire.

'Wasn't yesterday wonderful?' she said. I couldn't bear the distance and knelt at her feet, boldly taking her hand. She stroked my hair, and I leant on her knee while she talked of the

84

wonder of the new gift she'd experienced: the mumbo-jumbo Preacher John and she had been singing late last night was, she said, a Gift of the Holy Spirit, speaking in tongues. It was a sign of His second coming, she said, as I got hypnotised by the slow warmth of her hand on my head, mesmerised by the orange and mauve throbbing on the logs burning up in the fire. She turned my face towards her. Memories of Tess welled up like a crude postcard beside an old master.

'Did you feel it too?' she said, leaning towards me.

'Yes,' I said. The only thing could happen next was the kiss I'd been daring to dream of. She sat back and smiled.

'Let's have a toast,' she said serenely, squeezing my hand and rising. I relaxed in the warmth. She'd be back. And she was, holding two crystal goblets brimming with deep red wine. She arranged herself next to me on the carpet.

'Here's to you, Monica,' she said, raising her glass. 'You and me and all God's chillun.' She gave that adorable oh-shucks smile she always had when she talked American.

The deep slurred chime of glass rang in the air. I sipped, and tasted fruit rich with the memory of sunshine and the excitement of fermented bitterness. When I started to speak, she hushed me and we drank on in silence. I've drunk every kind of strong liquor this world can devise, and I swear I've never tasted anything so heady as this wine, this evening. She refilled our glasses, and the silence had become a game between us. We could smile, twinkle, grimace, sign with our hands, but words were out. Finally, when our glasses were empty, she shrugged at the bottle, and moved towards the door, beckoning me. I followed.

Oh my love, my honey, my only darling, I followed her up the stairs and she led me to my room. So it was to be here? I sat on my bed, and she made a show of turning back the covers and patting the pillow. Then she kissed my brow and whispered:

'If you can't sleep, I'm only next door.'

I watched her go and gazed at the closed door. Surely that was an invitation if ever I'd heard one? I pictured her, hair spread on the white linen: *Moonlight used to bathe the contours of your face/Wild chestnut hair fell all around the pillow-case* . . . But since we were playing the game of silence I waited until all in the house was still. I was almost asleep when she coughed. It was my signal. I crept across the room and eased the door open and stood motionless until the air had settled. I edged along the landing to her door, and drifted it open with my fingertips. I stood there, shivering. She turned in bed and saw me.

'Couldn't sleep?' she said, and her voice pulsed through the dark room.

'No,' I said, and sat on the edge of the bed. She reached out and held my hand. 'You're freezing! You'd better come in.'

In a second I was under the covers beside her, holding my shaking body firmly apart from her. What the hell was I supposed to do next?

'What's the matter?' she said, with such tenderness all I could do was dive into her arms, bury my face in her shoulder, racked with sobs and aching and longing all welling up like a river in spate. And so I clung to her, and gradually a heat built up in me like lying all day in the summer sun. I guessed I was supposed to do something else. She was magnificently still. I moved my shaking hand to her chin and stroked her cheek. Her strong hands moved through my hair. I kissed her chin and fumbled my way to her mouth. She kissed me back, strong, with closed lips. What next? I had read sex books. Erogenous zones – I felt like a clumsy fool as I nuzzled her ear-lobe. She held my head still.

'Oh, Monica, if it's making you feel like that,' she murmured with a kind of reproach. I subsided back to the warmth of her shoulder. It was enough. I cursed myself for my crudeness – she'd let me know when it was right to do more. I slept finally, and my last sight was the silver line curving along her cheek and lips.

I woke alone. She came in moments later and sat beside me.

'Last night must be a secret between us,' she said intensely, holding my hand. I kissed her fingers and her palm. She was my lady and her word was law.

10

Where I had been drifting before, now I was swimming with great gasps of oxygen to keep me afloat in this boundless ocean of love for Margaret. At school she was distant, which I respected, but back at her house we spent hours deep in each other's arms. It became a kind of dare with me to hug her closer, kiss her with all the passion I felt, and so long as I kept away from her mouth, she never objected. Sometimes she would detach my arms from her shoulders and laugh, protesting that we had work to do. I wrote more lyrically than I had dreamed I could and turned out at least a poem a day for her. I even tried my hand at stories and pictures. She said they were lovely.

I never questioned why a thirty-five-year-old deeply religious woman was fooling around with a passionate teenager like she was in love. I was in love with her, and she gave me no clear sign that she didn't feel the same. She said she loved me, she talked about us living together when we were deaf old ladies and had done all our exploring, like we belonged together. I knew I'd never find anyone who meant more to me, and so the time to the scholarship exam rocketed by, fuelled by this apocalyptic vision of our life. Leaving her had become a kind of medieval quest, whence I would return, truly worthy of her and covered with glory, all in her name.

I squared the religious side of it by thinking things like: *Our Margaret, who has brought me heaven on earth, hallowed be thy name.* It never struck me as sacrilegious. So Jesus hadn't chosen to speak to me in words like He'd done for Preacher John: He'd given me Margaret. My soul and heart were singing and I even found myself trying weird new harmonies when I was on my own, as if her Gifts of the Holy Spirit had become mine.

The night before the exam, we sat over the fire. I was

tantalised by how long I could last without throwing my arms round her.

'I've got something for you,' she said seriously, and handed me an envelope. I opened it – my first love letter? It was a folded piece of ivory-coloured paper, with red print and uneven typing all over it.

CERTIFIED COPY OF AN ENTRY OF BIRTH.
GIVEN AT THE GENERAL REGISTER OFFICE, LONDON
Registration District: Holdern-under-Ashe,
in the COUNTY BOROUGH of RUTLAND.

Then came my birth date in full. *Name, if any*, was followed by Noreen Jane. *Sex*: Girl. *Name and surname of father*: empty space. *Name, surname and maiden name of mother*: Rachel Emily Smith, Hospital Nurse of St Griselda, Holdern-under-Ashe, Rutland. *Occupation of father*: another empty space. A man with no name has no occupation – vile seducer? gas-station attendant?

I was registered nine days after my birth, and my mother's name was typed. Beyond the registrar's signature, G. K. Snellgrove, was a blurred and underlined word: *Adopted*. For this they'd brought in the big guns: Supt. Registrar, J. Davids.

'I hope you didn't mind,' said Margaret when I looked at her, 'I thought you'd be needing this when you go to England.'

She folded me in her arms. So I was Noreen Jane Smith after all. Not the name I'd have chosen, but it was mine. What the hell, I'd been Monica Robinson long enough not to like it. Monica was OK, but *Robinson*! That meant Pop. Monica Smith? Jane Robinson? I could be any damn permutation I chose.

'Better?' murmured Margaret.

It was better. I felt iron bars round my heart cracking, so close to her: *she* had given me this marvellous freedom. Even so, at bedtime, we started off apart. I went to her after a while, wanting only confirmation of our love, but she didn't ask me in. We talked a while and then she rose and tucked me back in my own bed.

'You've got a lot to do tomorrow,' she said, and left me.

But after the exam – after tomorrow, I knew she would no longer hold back and my cup would run over with sweetness. In the morning she gave me a rose, and me and Zip sat all day in this room, bare apart from a clock, a bored succession of teachers reading novels, and my glorious rose aglimmer with dew in a beaker on my desk. I'd finished while Zip was still frantically scribbling, and read through every word I'd written, tightening up a sentence here and there, pouring everything I knew of Margaret into the inevitable Jane Austen question. I had done what I could. And if I failed it would only mean I could move in with Margaret straight away and we could get on with our life.

The evening was marvellous: she poured wine liberally now that I didn't have to study any more for a while. We ate ribs in our hands, broke fresh-baked bread crunchy with seeds and dripping with golden butter; crisp chopped salad tangy with delicious dressing. Then she leaned back in her chair and asked me:

'What do you want, Monica? Right now. And in the future – you've got your life ahead of you, girlie, like an unmapped country.'

It was time to be frank. I had figured why should she lay herself on the line unless I did? I drank deep and kissed her fingertips.

'Right now, I want you,' I said, closing my eyes at my daring, 'I want us to be together for ever: Margaret, I want to give myself to you and have you as my own.'

I opened my eyes to see how she was taking it. What! She was looking really unhappy – had I been too gross, too sudden, too soon?

'What do you mean?' she said carefully, avoiding my burning eyes.

So I hadn't said *enough*!

'You know,' I said, 'We know how we feel. Other people may not agree, but it's nothing to do with them. Margaret, I've printed every word you've said on my heart, and I love you. You light up my life.'

There was a long silence. She added a log to the fire, and I picked up an awkwardness – something was wrong.

'I think,' she said slowly, 'that something's got very confused on the way. You sound as if you're talking about erotic love.'

The way she brought out those words made it sound like

leprosy. Our love, laid out on the dissection table? What was happening?

'Yes,' I said, trying to find familiar ground, 'I love you.'

'I love you too,' she said quickly. 'But – not like that.'

I began to feel like some disgusting biological specimen: *Observe the strange secretions from the primitive glands of this bizarre creature* . . . I was floundering.

'But —'

'The sort of love you are talking about,' she went on, suddenly the teacher faced with a bad assignment, 'is not the sort of love sanctioned by Our Lord. Some people feel it, but I believe that Satan has infected them.'

My diseased soul squirmed.

'Perhaps you'd better tell me more – I don't understand,' she went on.

I felt a quick flash of rage: what the hell did she mean, *I don't understand*? Hers was the hand that had clasped mine, hers the arms that had squashed the breath out of me; I had nuzzled at her neck, kissed her, even had her moaning in my arms one crazy afternoon. She had asked me to bed with her – hadn't she? YES SHE HAD! I was there! But maybe she had never done this before, I told myself, maybe she was a novice too.

I told her about Joanne Lee Hunter, and the first time I'd felt this all-consuming joy. That, she said with relief, was a teenage crush. Then I told her about Tess, editing it down to me refusing her animal passion, knowing that this was not Love. And then I fixed on her face and told her about *us*, and how clear and clean it all was for me since the moment she'd paused the car on that hairpin bend and held me close. I waited for affirmation.

She looked distressed, and swept her wonderful hair from her brow.

'Oh, Monica,' she said. 'Fools rush in where angels fear to tread! I can only say that I'm sure this is a phase. I hope there's nothing I've done to lead you to this perversion.'

Perversion? Infected by Satan? Margaret and me? I felt *us* crumble to foul dust in my hands. I hoped to God I'd got it wrong. But when I looked at her flushed face, her eyes closed on tears, I knew I hadn't.

I felt detached as I watched her. Was I supposed to deny this truth for her? If I was damned then let's hear it for the scarlet flames of the lost! I hoped to fuck I hadn't screwed up the scholarship exam. Phrases floated by me – I'd been flip, the way it was natural to me, tossing words away without a care, sure of myself, pass or fail. Jeez! If I had failed! And lost her, too! All I could do was thumb a ride out of this desolate place and see what happened.

'I'd better go to bed,' I said, unable to bear the agony on her face, the icy barrier around her. She nodded, and gave this heartbroken sob, waving me away and as I closed the living-room door, I heard her cross to the phone and dial. I stood stock still to listen. She was calling Preacher John and sobbing down the wires to him about her own fallibility. Oh, she could talk to *him*, all right! There were long silences when she only said yes, *yes*, and then she was speaking bible talk like she was giving responses in church. I knew this bitter night was not for sleeping, so I closed the front door behind me silently and flitted through the dark streets to Sam's, walling up my heart on the way. Perversion, huh? I'd better have a drink and get used to it.

'Well, goddam, Monica!' said Sam with genuine delight, about to close up for the night. 'How'd your scholarship exam go?'

'Wuz OK,' I said, lighting a cigarette. 'Gimme a drink, huh?'

Garbage to garbage, I tossed back the generous shot of moonshine. He grinned and refilled. Blackfoot Pete slouched from behind the counter.

'No place like home, huh?' he said, tapping a glass on the counter. Sam heh-hehed and poured us all another round. Clearly we were not about to head home and after a while he said nervously could he leave us to lock up? We nodded like two good old boys, he said to go easy and flip-flapped back to Doris.

'Well,' said Pete, straightening a creased cigarette from his pants pocket. 'To what do I owe the honour? I thought you'd have been in the lioness's den making whoopee, not dragged up here and looking lonesome.'

'Yeah,' I said, 'well I ain't, boy. Can you stand it?'

'My pleasure,' he said, passing the joint. 'Only I'd be obliged if you'd stop throwing sparks my way. Mine is not the fire nor yet, and I stress, *yet*, the flame!'

Damn! Even through his tangle of words I knew Pete knew me better than anyone. He'd had me sussed with my passion for Margaret and teased me obliquely for weeks. He fumbled the door locked and threw his arm carelessly round my shoulders as we stumbled back to his shack.

He lit incense like an anarchic priest, and rolled a joint while I sat and let the old moonshine surge through me.

'Billie Holliday?'

I nodded. He found a sassy tape, starting 'Baby, I don't cry over you' . . . I took in smoke as the Queen of the Blues put me right. *These foolish games you've been playing*. Well, I'd been the fool and she'd been playing games with me. *No man's a man enough to break my heart*.

I wrote in *woman* for man – what the hell, I'd been doing that ever since I could remember. Pete looked at me and shook his head.

'Don't let your bright circle wane, Monica my dear,' he said.

Then, after a long while, and like who-gives-a-damn:

'You want to screw or what?'

For God's sake! At least he didn't play the *touch me, touch me not* game. I started with guilt at this definition of Margaret and me. I didn't recognise the voice that said:

'Why the hell not?'

I could do with someone leaping on me for a change, a certainty, an end to this trembling *what next*? Pete smiled and said was he supposed to make all the moves? I told him yeah, with a fierceness that astonished me. He shrugged and moved to his knees in front of me. First he kissed me, and I tasted warm saliva, like Margaret had always held back from me. My body went on to a reckless automatic, and I held him tight like I was drowning. Why couldn't it be Margaret? Well, kid, I told myself, it ain't. And I was raging with hunger for heat.

'Now,' he said, striking a match, 'I'm supposed to climb on you and shove mah big *thang* inside you and hunca-hunca wham-bam thank you ma'am. However, that is the first step in making babies. I do not wish to make a baby. You do not wish to make a baby. No, no! So we have to improvise. Anyway, Monica, do I have you right – you're with the ladies on this?'

He sounded so serious. I said yes, I was with the ladies. As in satanically perverse, defined by Miss Margaret Courtland (MA Oxon.). I giggled. Margaret with all her God-squad shit was a million miles away from this natural warmth.

'Lie back,' he said intensely. 'This is not the best you'll get but it's the best you'll get from me. Take this damn cigarette. And if I get so I have to be inside you, I'll wrap it up. OK?'

Anything was OK. I lay back with the cigarette and Pete worked his mouth against my belly. I knew about fucking and wanted him to just *do it*, but he didn't. He buried his head between my thighs and I swear to God I could have died and gone to heaven. When I felt I was about to pass out he jack-knifed on top of me, grabbed something from the side of the bed, fumbled around with his hands and started to move inside me. God, it felt so good, like food after you've been starving all day. I wrapped myself round him and seconds later my whole head blew off. Jesus Christ! He lay back and slid his arm round me.

'Yeah,' he said, 'are you OK?'

I had no words. All at once, I was thinking of Margaret, about Tess, and cursed that it hadn't been with one of them. What the hell did Sue Ann mean by It ain't nothing to fret about? What the hell was Ted Bulstrode doing wrong? If I'd ever known what it was like I'd have been doing nothing else.

'Are you spending the night?' said Pete.

'Uh, no, I guess I ought to be at Margaret's place.'

'You're very welcome either way,' he said. 'Do what you want.'

I shivered my way into my clothes, said bye to Pete and walked through the streets to her door. I went in silently, went upstairs, got to bed, marvelling at my body, kind of weary and distant from all the agonising Margaret had chosen to do earlier.

I heard her get up, I heard her bathe, I heard her leave. Something in me died when she didn't wake me like she had so many times before. I lay and luxuriated in the pleasure my own hands could give me; I heard the school bell and dawdled over a shower and strong coffee. The day after a scholarship, I felt I was entitled to be late.

In the afternoon, there was Margaret, talking about John Donne. *Busie old foole, unruly Sunne!* Two lovers reluctant to meet the day. That could have been her and me. I sat and dared her to meet my eyes. She didn't. She said the poem was erotic and beautiful and I folded my arms and stared at her. Erotic was fine for poetry but not people. Huh! I worked Sam's all evening, caught a ride with Pop and even listened to him for once. I took my time saying good evening to Mom, fielded her moans and worries and told her I'd clear out the attic with her on Sunday.

'Ain't you going preaching with your friend?' she said shrilly.

'Nope,' I said, 'I've done the exam. Time I spent some time with my folks.'

Well, Mom being Mom, I couldn't expect enthusiasm. But she hummed and hawed and said it would be welcome to have a daughter and not a fly-by-night lodger. I even kissed her and Pop goodnight and went to bed, stashing my birth certificate in Pop's kitbag. Hell, I couldn't sleep. I went over to see Scoot. He was still crooning about his widder woman to give you joy! What about a bummed-out hippie and the end to charismatic bullshit; what about breathing clean after fine words and lofty ideas have bit the dust? We played cards and when I went back to the house about three I owed him three million bucks on a promissory note.

'I'll pay yuh!' I hollered through the trapdoor. 'Just let me make my fortune first!'

11

The Goldfish of God hailed me two weeks later bubbling about he hadn't seen me at the Discussion Group and how the Man Upstairs valued my contribution. I fended him off with talk of hard times at home. Well, I was now seven and a half billion in debt to my baby brother.

Zip Singer tried to corner me with earnest questions about the paper. I smart-talked him to silence. I hope he'd got the scholarship seeing as he wanted it so bad: I hoped I had too. The idea of organising my own way out of What Cheer was paralysing, especially now I was getting on OK with Mom and Pop.

Margaret never spoke to me direct, although I was there if she'd wanted. When the Principal announced my triumph in the scholarship in assembly, I felt for Zip, who was white with shame, and Margaret had her head bowed.

Huh!

Later that day I found an envelope in my locker and cursed the way my eager heart leapt into a Niagara of hope at the sight of Margaret's handwriting. My ability not to care was skin-deep – only say the word, and I shall be . . . *yours*? For all I jeered myself down, and cowboy-slouched away, the letter was burning in my pocket. What could she have to say to me now? I spread a few books out on a library table, and smoothed the single sheet down on one page.

My dear Monica,

I am delighted at the news of your scholarship and only wish I could have shared it with you first. I know that you especially will find England a great education and experience. It is unfortunate that Zachary won't be going with you, but I am sure that the Lord has other plans for him!

I *would* like to see you before you go. Perhaps you could come over to my house next Saturday about six for the evening? Let me know!

Love and best wishes, and CONGRATULATIONS!

Margaret

I read it, I learnt it by heart. So she did care! I daren't hope that she'd changed her mind since we last spoke. No, what I had offered her was a perversion, a work of Satan, and I couldn't see her going back on that. But if not . . . why did she want to see me? Maybe she had realised that it could be different for us? I'd only know by going. I left her a note thanking her for her kind invitation and saying I'd be glad to accept. Jane Austen couldn't have put it better.

I told Mom there was a little party in my honour, and she didn't say a word against it, except to wonder should I get myself a regular party dress. I pressed the fancy shirt I'd got in honour of Tess, and lashed out on some white chinos and fancy two-tone sneakers. Mom sighed and Pop roared and said danged if his li'l gal din' have her own style! He dug out a tooled leather belt with a silver buckle of intertwined hearts.

'I won that thang twenty-three years back at the Valentine Ball in Evenin' Shade!' he boasted. 'You recall, Kathereen? They give you an orchid for your pretty hair, seein' as we danced so good! You enjoy your party, baby!'

We had to punch new holes in the belt, and even Mom said I looked good. Scoot drove me to What Cheer, glad of a double excuse to get the wagon for the evening. I told him I might be staying over, and he grinned and gave me a number where I could reach him in the morning at the widow's house. I went into Sam's to get a little courage to face Margaret. Pete and Sam both whistled at me, and wouldn't hear of me paying for a drink. Pete feigned tragedy when I said I wasn't staying long. I figured to get to Margaret's around six-thirty, give *her* a while to worry for a change.

I drained my glass and left at six twenty-five, cooling myself down on the walk for whatever she might throw my way. I had a small bottle of moonshine in my bag, just in case. She opened the door with a radiant smile like we'd never argued and everything was like it always had been. She took my hand.

How could I ever have doubted her? She led me to the closed living-room door, then flung it wide and drew me inside.

For Chrissake! The room was full – every kid from the Christian Discussion Group was there, smiling fit to beat the band and cheering me! The ripple of clapping hit my brain like a headache.

'We're so glad for you, Monica,' said Lily MacMahon, 'and we'd like you to have this to remember us by!'

They'd given me a signed framed photo of all of them, with Margaret and Reverend Taylor Hadley standing in the centre like proud parents. I thanked them, my wicked heart pulsing with the desire to scream at Margaret with all of them there, denounce her once and for all. Goddam, she was clever! She knew I'd never have come if I'd known it wasn't to be just her and me; she knew I'd shunned the group since she'd shunned me. This little gathering would make her feel better. *We gave her a good send-off, didn't we?* Jeez, old Preacher John had probably masterminded the whole idea on one of their long-distance heart-search conversations.

When I looked at the group something else struck me: there was Lily and Ralph, Marianne and Huey, Charlotte and Houston, Mary Belle and Scot, even Sue Ann and Ted: it went boy/girl, girl/boy, boy/girl all around the room till it got to Zip Singer. And there was me. And then there was Margaret. She was busy ladling out fruit cup and handing round sandwiches, the perfect hostess, but not to this girl. I asked her if there was anything stronger and she looked very serious for a moment and said no, like I was some kind of freak.

I felt denied. I had chosen to quit the group and here they were by her *invitation*. She and I had drunk deep of good red wine and held each other close in all those hours alone, and now I was to sip fruit cup and make polite conversation in Christian company. Lawdy me! I could have brought my grandmother to this gathering, suppose I'd had one living. People sat or stood in little groups, apart from Zip who was alone by the window, crimson and miserable.

'Go and talk to Zachary,' Margaret murmured over my shoulder. 'He's feeling very bad.'

And why the hell not? If she could act ministering angel to

the lost and lonely, then I could be a fucking chameleon against the flowered curtains.

'Hey, Zip,' I said, 'Cheers!'

'Cheers, Monica,' he stammered, gulping his punch and coughing.

'Look, I'm real sorry you didn't get the scholarship,' I said, and meant it. 'What're you going to do?'

God, he was a bundle of nerves! While he groped for words, I noticed this odd quietness in the room – every damn ring-fingered couple in the room was watching us like they weren't really, and Margaret was close to Lily and Ralph, casting a glance our way like some mother hen. I felt like one of those Chinese giant pandas supposed to be getting it on with a total stranger from across the globe, with the world's press logging every move. Damned if we hadn't been set up! I could just see it Margaret's way. She'd gone on at me about boyfriends often enough, and I'd told her my views. She'd probably decided I needed to meet a suitable young man to get rid of my unnatural attachment to her. She was playing God with my life again, sweeping aside everything about me that didn't fit the holy bullshit blueprint of Monica Robinson. I wished savagely that I'd swanned in here with Pete on my arm, trailing clouds of sweet-scented smoke and smiling like the devil incarnate. Damn her! Damn her to the hell she'd chosen to drop me in!

Later she put the radio on a dance-tune station and people obediently started to dance. Margaret came over to where Zip and I were examining the carpet and said how were we getting on and wasn't it nice to have a chance to talk? I caught her eye and held it. How dare she! Zip said it was a lovely party, but he'd have to get home soon.

This didn't fit with Margaret's plans, nor did the way other people started to drift off around ten, thanking her so much! She practically begged them to stay, but by ten-thirty the room was empty, except for me and her. I sat down, like I was the most relaxed person in the world. She moved around clearing up, it was like a game: could she keep a piece of furniture between us at every point? She could!

Finally, there was nothing else for her to fiddle with, and she sat on the edge of a chair opposite me. I stared at her face, waiting for her eyes to meet mine.

Had I enjoyed myself?

Wasn't the photo a nice gesture?

Had I had a chance to talk to Zachary and wasn't he a nice young man?

Yes, Margaret. Yes, and Yes again.

Followed by silence.

And then she started talking nervously, quickly.

'I feel that perhaps I over-reacted when I saw you last. It was such a surprise to me – so much passion, Monica. Of course, I am very fond of you.'

I figured there was nothing to answer while she skated around this way. What of our plans to live together when we were old? What of our hungry silent embraces? Very fond! *Wake up, sister*, I mouthed.

'When do you leave?' she asked.

'Next week.'

'A whole new chapter,' she said.

And what of our plans to take the plane to New York together? Not a word. Mom had shaken her head and said they could about make the bus fare, but as for planes – no way! When Margaret had said she'd love to come and see me off, I'd figured it was worth blowing some of my savings on a plane ticket, for the sheer joy of my first flight being with her. Now I knew she wouldn't come with me, I decided the bus was just my style. Rural American. Cheap and cheerless.

'Well, I have an early start tomorrow,' she said suddenly. My marching orders. When I didn't jump up immediately, she added, 'You can't stay here, Monica. It's not a good idea.'

'I'm not stuck for a bed for the night,' I said coldly, standing, 'I'm going, don't worry. I guess this is goodbye.'

'Goodbye,' she said. She'd got a chair between me and her, suppose I was about to do something gross and perverted like touch her. The leprosy of lesbianism.

'Can I make a call?' I said.

She nodded and went into the kitchen. I punched the number Scoot had given me. A woman's voice answered. Then Scoot came on.

'Any chance of a ride tonight, bro? If not, that's fine, I have an alternative.' I figured I could use Pete's couch, but I'd rather not.

'God, that's terrible,' said Scoot like there'd been a death in the family, 'I'll be right over, Monica. Don't you worry.'

I heard the same woman's voice shrill what-the-hell-was-all-that-about as I put down the phone. I polluted the sanctified living-room with one of Pete's sweet and sinful joints. The plague of my presence kept Margaret corralled in the kitchen till I heard the truck toot outside.

On the way home, Scoot fell over himself thanking me for the call. The widder woman was getting a little tedious about a ring, he said, and when I said sure she was, what did he expect messing around, he rubbed his hand on his jeans and sighed.

'Thing is, I don't want to settle down, Monica,' he said. 'It ain't her. She's a good woman. It's me. It's about time I quit jackassing around this no-good county and hit that old road. I'm more fond of her than any woman I've known. She's even got a little kid and he's swell. But I ain't gonna be no daddy till I decide. Only decent thing I can do is leave. When're you off?'

'Next week,' I said. 'And not a day too soon.'

'I better leave it a couple of months to hush up Mom,' said Scoot. 'Damn, I want to pick up and go right now.'

'Do it,' I said. 'Just do it. You wait for the right day and it'll never come.' And when you think it has, baby bro, you're probably going to be as wrong as your smart sister. I didn't say it. He'd find out fast enough anyway.

The week flew by. I packed up Pop's kitbag, and resisted all Mom's suggestions that we should go shopping. I had enough to kit myself out in England and what I'd heard when it wasn't raining there, it was snow or fog. I figured they'd have better clothes to fit their own crazy weather than Miss Eliza's Quality Clothing Emporium.

My last morning, I shucked on Tess's shirt and a clean pair of jeans and said my goodbyes.

Mom didn't want to come to the bus. Pop said he'd drop me off and be right back.

'You write, you hear?' said Mom. 'And come back before I'm too old and foolish to recognise you. Now git!'

I hugged her and she near broke my back in return. Truth to tell, I was a litle tearful too. I'd given myself a good hour for the bus, and when Pop had driven off, pressing 50 bucks into my hand for the trip, I squared myself and strolled deliberately to

Margaret's. Well, my feet took me that way. My feet and my aching heart, though my pride raged and jeered at me for a fool. I just had to give us one last chance.

She asked me in, and there was a girl two years my junior sitting in the living-room. Poor sap, I felt for the anxious look on her face. Margaret's next casualty? I asked for coffee, though Margaret offered me tea. I was leaving all this behind me. I heard Margaret using the same thrilling phrases she'd got me with. And each one she said like she'd just thought of it. As I left, she gave me a parcel, with instructions not to open it until I was in the air. No problem to me: I might just leave it wrapped, or throw it away at some unnamed bus stop. To the last minute I was hoping in a weary trembling way that she'd declare herself, give me a reason to hope, but we parted with a handshake, a sliding away of her eyes. It was over, and for her, It had never been.

Six years too late and finally I was headed in the same direction as Joanne Lee Hunter: north. I couldn't even picture her face any more. And the bus I was in hailed from the same era as her parents' half-timbered estate car: it was no greyhound, this vehicle, more like the family dog that spends half its life dozing on the doorstep. I took the second seat from the back, and smeared myself a porthole to watch America slouching by.

The seat in front of mine was crowned with peroxide curls and a fitful cloud of smoke. About twenty miles on, when I'd seen enough dust and tumbleweed to get the general idea, a brown-eyed child popped up from the other seat and stared at me.

'Giddown there, Rudi,' came whining through the smoke.

Rudi's hands clamped to the seat-back, and he hooked his chin over. I swear children never blink. He stuck out his tongue at me. I made the kind of face that used to send Scoot screaming to Mom. This kid giggled, and rolled both eyes right in, lolling his tongue. We swapped Lon Chaney impressions for a while, then he disappeared. I lit a cigarette.

Now his Mom turned and craned over the seat.

'He ain't been botherin' you none?'

'No.'

'You got a cigarette? I got the wrong bag with me. I can get some when we stop up ahead.'

'Sure,' I said, passing her the pack.

'Y'see,' she threw half over her shoulder, 'we been going all night. I could use some company.'

'Sure,' I said.

She crossed over Rudi and plumped down next to me. Her cotton dress was travel-creased, and her bright pink powder was sweated right through.

'You stretch out, baby, and git some sleep,' she told Rudi. His face slid out of view.

'Name's Etta Casucci. Goin' far?'

'Monica Robinson. I'm going north,' I told her.

'North,' she said, 'Goddam. Rudi's Pop moved up north a while back, and finally got to sending for us. I guess he's run out of clean shirts and gotten sick with cafeteria food. But he says he's fixed up a couple of rooms real nice, got a three-piece on the never-never. Chocolate-brown moquette.'

'Uh-huh,' I said.

'Long as we don't have to change again,' she said darkly. 'We had to git out in the middle of the night, being as there was an accident. I got no clear idea where they dug this bus out of. It don't seem fit to go more than fifty miles, and we done nigh on two hunnerd already. Damned if I couldn't use some coffee. You know what? Rudi's Pop's got one of them stainless steel percolators now in the new apartment. I said I wouldn't move unless he got a percolator, a deep-freeze and a tumble-dryer out of the catalogue. I had a lovely home down in Gatorville. Shame to lose it, but it come with the job, and they started pumping some kinda shit into the river down there, and wasn't no more alligators to kill and skin being as they was all dead. God, you shoulda seen the way I fixed that place up . . .'

An age later I felt I knew every sunflowered tile in the kitchen, all the matching sets of dinner-mats in the kitchen-diner, and each square of Kiddi-Pruf carpet in little Rudi's bedroom. He had walls papered with E.T., a Transformers mobile, and every He-man toy in the catalogue from Buzzoff to the full-scale Castle of Greyskull. They'd had to go back when the payments stopped and only the fact that Etta'd stuck the

102

paper to the walls stopped the repo man making off with that too.

Then the bus squelched to a halt, and stood shuddering and steaming outside Lauren's KOF-E-SPOT.

'This ain't no scheduled stop,' said Etta.

'Gotta check out the moving parts here. Half an hour, folks,' drawled the driver, yanking at the engine cover. He vanished in a cloud of steam. Etta shrugged and we hauled ourselves over to the bleached board shack perched on the flat landscape like it had been dropped out of the sky. Lauren had a row of off-white china mugs lined up on the marbled formica counter top, and trailed the coffee-pot from one to the next without a pause.

'Kid want milk? Cola? What?'

'He can't keep milk down,' said Etta. 'Give me a Coca-Cola.'

'Cola, honey, it ain't Coke. We don't git no folks needing the real thing out here.'

The same went for the coffee. Etta mourned the percolator waiting for her in some set of two rooms some 300 miles away. We pushed the spoons around the grey-brown liquid, and stared outside where the driver was shaking his head over the engine. Up the road was the same as down the road. Nothing. So this was travelling. Margaret had enthused when she knew I was going – *keep a diary!*

Dear Diary, Today I gave up all hope of love and passed through a thousand miles of barren dirt from horizon to horizon.

'Monica, what in the hell's that?' Etta was squinting against the glare at a distant puff of dust with a mirage of dark figures at the centre. The noise came first: the shrieking raw muscle of big bikes. Three helmeted figures swept around the bus and drew up in line outside the window. Leather ridged with dust and eyes obliterated by mirror-shades.

'God save us!' said Etta, drawing Rudi to her. Lauren came from behind the counter, her face blank like a cat woken too early. The three figures swaggered up to the cafe door, and hauled off their helmets as they came in. Two wild beards, one brown, one grey, and a firm-jawed woman. They stood staring at Lauren.

'Well I'll be goddammed,' said Lauren. 'To what do I owe the honour? Think your ma might have died, and come back to hear the will read, huh?'

'Maw,' said the younger beard.

'Knew we'd be back some day, didn't you?' said the woman, and bear-hugged Lauren.

'You damned kids. Quit squashing me, Maureen,' growled Lauren. 'And who's your friend?'

'This is Billy, Maw, we been riding together.'

'Hi, Billy,' said Lauren, shaking his awkward gauntlet. She settled the three of them in front of coffee and pie.

'You got a lot of custom,' said Maureen, nodding at the half busload hunched around the room. Lauren shrugged massively.

'It's Ben. Figures to drive that bus right up north. Today. I know that bus. You kids oughtta know that bus. Took us up to Michigan camping when you wasn't but twelve, Maureen. They oughtta retired it years back. Like I oughtta be enjoying my old age on a beach somewhere, laying under a palm-tree, instead of waiting for a bunch of ungrateful kids to come home and take care of me. Huh. Me and that bus go back some. Neither one of us going to have a retirement. Work till you drop, and lay where you fall. How long you stayin'? Where you headed?'

'We just come down for a few days to see you, Maw,' said her son.

'And?'

'And nothin'. Can't a family visit with their Maw?'

'Jesus,' said Lauren. 'I'd buy that from Maureen, but you, Spencer? Every time I seen your feet through my door these past ten years I only got one question. How much?'

'Spencer's doing real well up north,' said Billy. 'Workin' in my repairs shop. Boy don't need no handouts.'

'It'll be the first time,' said Lauren.

The bus driver pushed the screen door open, and came in.

'Coffee, Ben?' said Lauren.

'I could use a coffee, Lauren, but I'll be ding-dong-daddioed if I know what that damn bus needs to keep her on the road! She's been running on a wish and a prayer since Saint Gervaise, and every state line we come to I can feel her whole guts shudder like she'd been supping green water. I got to get these folks as good as four hunnerd miles north, Lauren, and the bus just don't have the heart for it.'

Lauren shrugged and said there was fold-up beds out the back if it came to it. I felt panicky: I had a plane to catch.

12

I watched the evening sun go down. Etta and Rudi were sleeping sprawled uncomfortably across two chairs. Ben was fiddling with the engine still, with Billy standing beside him. Every so often Ben would stand up and shake his head, and Billy would shrug. I felt paralysed. The final blasting irony: Monica Robinson blows her scholarship by missing the plane. So? I didn't want to go, anyhow. I didn't really want to do anything, except maybe be a hobo, turn myself into a freight-train hopper crazy old bag-lady, wandering through life with tatty parcels tied with string. A woman like that had gone through What Cheer some years ago, and her face lit up only when she found a cigarette butt and stowed it in her filthy coat pocket. Who the hell cared anyhow?

Ben clipped a light on to the engine hood and carried on for a half-hour or so. I drank more coffee. Then he closed the engine, and came into the cafe. I reached for my bag. We were off again!

'It ain't good,' he said. 'The bus ain't safe to travel on, specially at night. I'd hate for you folks to freeze to death in the middle of nowhere. We'd better stop the night here, and I'll have a man come over with spares first thing.'

'Oh, Jesus!' wailed Etta. 'Once last night I called my man to say we'd be late – I gotta call again tonight? What's he going to think? Mister, this ain't right.'

'I'm truly sorry, ma'am, but there's not a thing I can do about it.'

'I have a plane to catch,' I said.

'Fraid you'll have to get the next one, miss,' said Ben.

'I'm supposed to be going to England,' I said.

'We'll do our best to get there,' he said, and patted my

shoulder. I felt like snarling at him to keep his paws to himself. He had the same reassuring way with him as my Pop.

'I can fix up beds for you folks,' said Lauren, 'and supper too.'

Ben smiled at her gratefully, against the murmur of complaints and resignation in the room.

'England? You're going to England?' said Etta.

'Yeah,' I said. 'At least, I thought I was.'

'Oh, that's too bad,' she said. 'I better go and see where to put Rudi for sleeping. I better get on the phone. You better book yourself another flight, honey.'

I had the feeling the Lady Constance Glynn Scholarship Foundation would not take well to a scholar goofing it up before she even got there. Besides I didn't care to make the effort. Goddam, I found a sour smile settle on my face as I recognised my silly heart still hoping for a reconciliation with Margaret, still believing things would work out, like a fly buzzing at the invisible fact of a glass window-pane.

'Hi there.'

It was Maureen, Lauren's daughter, minus leather jacket. She was a broad-shouldered woman, not the type you'd argue with. But she was giving me a real friendly smile.

'Can I join you?' I nodded and she sat across from me, pushed a glass my way and slipped in a neat shot of bourbon from a silver flask.

'Going any place special?' she asked. Her voice was light, but I felt I recognised something about her. Her brown eyes said a lot more than I could work out.

'I have to catch a plane tomorrow for England,' I said, 'I'm on a scholarship. Supposed to be.'

'Can you change the flight?'

'Hell, I don't know.'

'What kind of scholarship?'

'English. Literature,' I threw out like I didn't care. Which I didn't.

'Sheee-it! That's tough,' she said. 'The phone out back's jammed with Mr and Mrs US of A calling the folks. You better try later.'

'Well, I guess it'll be OK,' I said.

'Ben's kinda sweet on Lauren. He's been hanging round this

107

place since I was a kid. She won't have no truck with him, but he ain't the boy to give up. He's got no hurry to leave. Every goddam trip he wangles this way the bus breaks down. He can spin it out over days, honey. You wanna beer? You wanna play pool while you think what to do?'

Maureen racked up the rainbow of balls and chalked her cue. She played fast, and she played good. All she said through the game was *shot!* and *tough luck!* Before she made her shots, she took a quick puff on her cigarette, and dipped into her beer, then eyed down the cue. A neat and perfect thwack! every time. I guessed I'd better make that call, though I was quite content to be here, now.

'I'll get the beers,' she said.

But there was no answer to the Lady Constance Foundation contact number. If I'd kindly leave my name and number, they'd get back to me. But no one would be available to take my call until tomorrow evening. And then it would be too late. Big deal. I hung up on the parrot screech of the tone and rejoined Maureen.

'No dice?' she asked.

I shook my head.

Our scores were even when Lauren called everybody through for supper. She made a few long-suffering digs at Maureen about girls who just didn't give a damn if their Mom was to die slaving over a stove. She added that she'd got a bed for me, if I *happened* to be interested. At this she glared at Maureen just like my Mom's deal-with-you-later look. She sure was sore about something.

'Goddam woman!' snorted Maureen as we sat and ate. 'Nag, nag, bitch and guilt trip when I'm here and then I get fuck only knows what shit when I don't come home more often. Always!'

I didn't understand the ins and outs of it all and figured it was none of my affair anyhow. Anyone fool enough to try and work out what goes on between people in a family is asking for trouble. I couldn't even work out my own.

After supper, we went back to the pool table. For politeness' sake, we played a couple of guys, but I could have lived without their assumptions about 'young ladies' needing advice on how to hold a cue and the angle of every shot. Then Lauren glowered round the door that she'd show me my bed.

'No need, Ma,' said Maureen, 'I'll do that.'

'You better,' Lauren was threatening. '*Her* bed, mind.'

I suddenly had a flash of recognition. Yeah! Something in Maureen's raunchy gusto brought Tess to mind. I sneaked a look at her. She was flashing daggers at Lauren, her chin set and her feet planted apart.

'Say goodnight, Lauren,' she warned.

'You're still my kid, and this is my roof you're under,' said Lauren, 'What you do away from me I don't even care to think about, but when you're here – Maureen, I'm telling you!'

'Good night, Lauren,' said Maureen, and stared at her mother until she left us alone. Then she chalked her cue and muffed every shot for the rest of the game.

'Damn woman can still upset me,' she grumbled with a pained, forced grin, 'Hell, I need some air. You wanna walk?'

We walked into the night-time desert, swinging cans of beer, pausing to light cigarettes. I thought of the time I'd stumbled along with Tess in the dark. It seemed like years ago. I was a thousand per cent more sober now; besides, I didn't feel like that about Maureen. I was curious as hell, but I guess people tell you what they want you to know. I was not about to pry. We slowed naturally away from the lighted shack, and sat down on a rock.

'I have to apologise for the floor show,' said Maureen. 'Shit! Lauren can really play a number when it suits her. I've been out with her for five years, she even met the last woman I was with, and she still thinks I'm only waiting for the right man.'

Sounded familiar. Christ! I'd never even thought about telling my Mom about the weird feelings I had for women. She'd throw me out of the house at least! Besides, I felt it had nothing to do with her. If I was dating some yoyo guy I'd never have told her either. I had a sense she'd find fault with whoever I chose.

'Honey, I'm making some gross judgements here!' said Maureen, 'I got this mouth that just goes and goes – how dare I presume you're a dyke!! I guess it's just that you look like one. You act like one. You are, aren't you?'

Dyke. I liked the word and I liked the way she said it with relish. I guessed it meant the way I felt about women. With the stars above me and beer cool and foaming in my mouth, I raised my can to the darkness – I was a dyke.

'Yeah,' I said, and it made my heart beat fast and strong.

'You got a lover in England?' said Maureen.

'Not yet,' I said, trying to match her tough cool.

'You leaving a lover? You got that don't-give-a-shit look, honey. *What becomes of the broken hearted . . .?* Am I right?'

I was glad for the night hiding the way my face tightened to stop the tears.

'Big one, huh?' said Maureen, squeezing my hand. 'You wanna talk about it?'

I threw together the story of me and Margaret as sparsely as I could and as angry as it made me feel.

'Well, screw the stupid bitch,' said Maureen. 'And here's to the day you stop caring. That'll be a good day, believe me. You don't believe it'll ever come, the way you feel now, but I'm telling you, without pulling age and experience, you'll get over it. And when that time comes, honey, it's like losing a ball and chain.'

'Janis Joplin?' I said.

'Aw, darlin' fuckhead Janis. She was a dyke, you know.'

'Janis *Joplin*?' Hell, she was a *star*!

'Oh, yeah, sweet Janis. Should have stuck to women and skipped the fuckin needle. Fuckin smack destroying her body and a bunch of pisshead pricks destroying her mind. Parasites!'

This was new to me. Pete had lovingly outlined Janis' lifelong heartbreak looking for one good man; all her songs said the same. But Maureen sounded like she knew what she was talking about. And I liked the idea that I was cut from the same cloth as Janis and her arc-welder voice.

'You wanna walk some more? I'm not ready to face mommie dearest back there yet,' said Maureen, snapping her can and tearing the thin metal. I drained mine, we lit cigarettes and walked with our backs to the shack.

'I'll tell you what,' said Maureen, 'I only came down this way cuz Spencer was shit-scared to make it on his own. Billy's his boyfriend, and he had this nuts idea about taking him home to meet Momma. I got nothing here besides dark looks and sermonising. I'll take you to the airport. I'd rather be back in good old sin-filled decadent NY anyhow. OK?'

110

What was I to say? *Oh, no! I couldn't possibly put you to all that trouble!* I liked the idea. And Spencer had a boyfriend? Guys felt like this about their own kind as well as women? Jeez!

'I'd really like that,' I told her.

'It's a deal,' she said. 'If we set off before sun-up we'll get a clear run through. Should have time for a drink too, before you get into the big white bird. I never been to England myself.'

'Come and visit,' I said.

She laughed, kind of pleased.

'I might just do that,' she said.

There was a new peace in the darkness. We stopped, and had this really close hug, body to body. I liked this Maureen and her firm warmth, the strength in her arms around me. And I knew she liked me too.

Back at the house, the cafe lights were down. We tiptoed through the gloom, and Maureen gripped my arm at the doorway. She jerked her head at a closed door. Lauren was giving out to someone.

'You come down here grinning like a fool and tell me this and I'm supposed to be happy! Spencer, I gave you birth and I raised you, and I hoped to make you the man your foolish father never was. I have to put up with your sister turning unnatural and dragging trollops down here and shaming her Maw, and now I got to have my boy bringing diseased perverts back home! God knows I always lived right. I kept my name pure for you kids' sake after they took your Pop away, and what did it bring me? A daughter strutting round in pants like a man! A goddam pansy son with an earring, hanging round with a man old enough to be his father! Yeah, I'm talking to you, mister, leading my boy into sin. Working with you? I'd like to know what you perverts call work! I got a good idea.'

'You got a dirty mind, lady,' said Billy. We heard a plate shatter against the wall, and Lauren start screaming. *Home, home on the range!*

Maureen led me up many stairs and to a room where she closed and locked the door.

'I figure Spencer told Maw,' she said, gritting her teeth, 'Jesus, half her time she's complaining that we don't come home and when we are here she's driving us away. Shit! I guess

111

it's bedtime. Hey – I never asked you – you wanna sleep in with me?'

'Sure,' I said. Whatever. As if she had to ask

I had to giggle as she threw on a night-dress, baby-blue cotton and broderie anglaise at the neck. She looked about twelve years old. I always slept in T-shirts, myself. I'd have felt funny and wrong in the kind of thing she was wearing. But she looked lovely, kind of soft and sweet.

I got into bed. She slid in beside me, and we lay looking at the ceiling. What was I feeling? Curious, amd kind of excited. I'd never slept with a woman before, apart from that kiss-and-don't-tell night with Margaret. This felt so much easier. Maureen wound her alarm, and turned the light out. It was the most natural thing in the world when our arms went round each other, our toes rubbed together, and this stupendous, sure, mild warmth crept through me like an early June day with the sun just rising. I lay and luxuriated, with her breath on my cheek. Her face was so soft, and her lips nudged this gentle open-ended kiss on to mine.

'Well, ain't this nice?' she murmured, stroking my shoulders.

'Mm,' I said, and felt the lovely solid muscle in her arm. She stroked my face. I stroked her face. I felt like a wondering baby. This was all new to me. We touched each other for hours with this tender delight. She stroked my breasts like she'd found a treasure, and I smiled in the dark as my fingers found the smooth curve of her breast. Godalmighty, she felt so wonderful. This strange flesh, heated by her heartbeat. I wanted to just dive down and nuzzle at her nipples, my fingertips were too far away. Could I? But already her face was rubbing against my neck, and her lips fastened on my breast. I held her head like it was a fragile bird's egg. Who'd have believed that a tough, strong woman could have hair like down? And then we hugged again, and touched from head to foot, soothed and oh, how we fit each other! I edged aside her ridiculous night-dress and found her breast. She drew the covers over my head, and cradled me against her. It was OK, it was fine, it was good, it was the best, my face hot against her, my tongue and lips drinking her in.

We slept. In the night, I turned and wrapped my arms round her back, and she snuggled back into my lap, holding my hand.

And later we both turned over and I slept in the shelter of her warm body.

And then it was morning, and she woke me with a hug.

'I've killed the alarm,' she whispered. 'We'll have to sneak out real quiet. I don't wish to have the neighbourhood disturbed by my mother's opinion of me.'

Dressing was silent giggle time. We padded down the stairs like Laurel and Hardy, and only breathed easy outside. I put my shoes on, and Maureen wrapped a thick jacket round me and handed me a helmet.

'That all you got?' she said, tying my bag on the bike.

'Yeah.'

'Travelling light, huh?'

I smiled into the dawn-streaked sky. All the lighter for meeting you my dear, all the better for sleeping, simply sleeping, in your arms.

'OK,' she said. 'Hop on.'

I straddled the sleek great machine, and Maureen slammed it into life.

''Ats mah baby!' she shouted above the engine and we wheeled a spray of red dirt past the dead bus and hit the road. I gripped my arms round her, and squinted into the new day. I felt so safe with her, and this grin just kept on coming. I felt like I could ride with her for ever.

We stopped just after sun-up, to unfreeze over coffee and doughnuts, cigarettes and coffee.

'OK?' said Maureen, with a sugar-lipped grin.

'OK.'

We went on, stopped for gas, stopped for more coffee.

By the time we hit the eight-lane highway looping round the Emerald City glitter of New York, so had the rest of the wheeled population of the world. I'd never seen so much traffic. The way Maureen cruised the big bike through the sweltering lanes took my breath! I felt we'd come off the road in a different vehicle, with different heads and bodies as we skimmed past juggernauts, flipped across Mercedes Benz fenders, grazed the high-gloss limo doors. Then we took a right and plunged down off the freeway to the canyons of the streets, cliffs of mirrored glass and concrete cutting out all but a wedge of sky.

And the people! Scuttling across at the lights, jay-walking, hawking exotic trays on street corners; a fur-collared old lady tugging at a pooch in a fur jacket; a group of black guys eight foot tall, just hanging around; a whole army of pastel-skirted women in sensible jackets milling in and out of buildings. New York City!

We roared out of the teeming streets through unreal neon in a wide, howling tunnel and burst into dazzling daytime a world away from shops and houses. Maureen jerked her hand at a sign suspended over the roller-coaster road: JOHN F. KENNEDY AIRPORT.

I crammed my head over her shoulder and read the time. I was already late. That drink would have to wait till I came back, or till she came to see me. We wheeled into the lane marked INTERNATIONAL DEPARTURES.

She bumped the bike to a halt outside glass doors a mile wide.

'I ain't shit at goodbyes,' she said. 'Get outta here – write me, y'hear!'

13

I slid off Maureen's bike and took off the helmet, my head ringing with the speed. I unhooked the kitbag and waved as she roared away. She raised one gauntlet and was gone. I stood for a moment, then turned. The glass doors parted and I felt like a Martian as they slid closed behind me.

I wanted to run away the moment I spotted my group. They were not my kind and I felt more alien the closer I got. Mostly women, lip-glossed simpers and matching suits, patent-leather shoes and clutch bags. They were all wearing bright yellow buttons saying LADY CONSTANCE GLYNN SCHOLARSHIP FOUNDATION. Crocodile rubbed up against initialled pigskin in the carefully stacked luggage trolleys. Shit! Where did I put that dumb-ass button? To hell. I sauntered over and let my canvas sack slump beside the scads of hand-cured opulence. A navy-suited woman with a clipboard looked me up and down. She had a square name-tag clipped through her lapel: Mrs Eleanor Weiss.

'This is the Lady Constance Glynn Scholarship Foundation.' Polite, but dismissing the possibility of my having any place in the well-heeled coterie.

'I'm Monica Robinson.'

She scanned the list and whipped out a steel pen.

'Monica Robinson. You're not wearing your button. And we did ask you to be here three hours prior to departure.'

'I had a few transport problems,' I said, and she made a mark on her board.

There were five clones of the boy next door, with knitted ties knotted tight around their earnest throats. They wore identical tweed jackets and straight pants and the fashionable equivalent of a crew-cut.

'HEY, MONICA! DAMNED IF I DIDN'T THINK I'D MISS YOU!'

Maureen puffed over to me, shaking her sweat-soaked hair.

'You forgot your goddam button, honey!'

Of course, I'd pinned it to her jacket this morning as we giggled our way on to the road after a coffee stop.

'Jeeeee–zuzzz!' she looked at the group and burst out laughing. 'I'll leave you to it! You have a good time, you hear! Write me!'

I hugged her good and proper and turned to read *monster* on every refined scholarship face. Mrs Eleanor Weiss was scrutinising the crowd with alarm.

'I'm very concerned,' she twittered. 'Miss Robinson, you were late, but Mr LaSalle! Heavens! He's two hours overdue!'

'Mrs Weiss?' drawled a peachy-blonde, all elegance and languish, 'would it be *all* right with you if me and Melinda got us some coffee? I don't imagine we'd find iced tea in New York. Me and Melinda have been standing here since nine this morning! I'm parched!'

She looked at me pointedly.

'Well, Miss — er —'

'Rous*seau*. Rosamund Rous*seau*. Me and Melinda were the first to register. Melinda Bishop.'

'Of course, girls, get yourselves some coffee. In fact,' she clapped her hands, 'all of you young folk could go and wait for me in the cafeteria. This is unpardonable! I shall wait for Mr LaSalle.'

Ms Rous*seau* and Ms Bishop led the merry throng away. I felt obligated to stay, being as I was so late and couldn't have stomached coffee with Southern Belles and preppies on the side. Mrs Weiss was starting to panic.

'There's always one,' she told me. 'One who simply cannot be punctual. I've been escorting students for the Lady Constance Foundation for twenty years and every year one of you turns up as the gates are closing.'

'What time is the plane?'

'Miss Robinson, I sent you the schedule. As well as the button. Boarding commences at 12.30. The plane departs at 1.30.'

It was 12.10. Mr LaSalle was cutting it fine.

'I'll wait for him, if you want to get some coffee, Mrs Weiss,' I said, trying to absolve myself.

'Thank you, no,' she said, like I was a kleptomaniac offering to mind the shop. I sat on Pop's kitbag and lit a cigarette. Mrs Weiss coughed and moved away.

'It is not as if Mr LaSalle had far to come,' she said fretfully. 'He only lives in Baltimore. Oh, whatever's this?'

'This' was six roller-skating young men with blond movie good looks racing towards us in lamé pants. Followed by a theatrically costumed entourage of movie goddesses, Greek temple attendants, extras from a Marlon Brando bike movie, James Dean clones and a bevy of Canadian lumberjack moustaches. They stopped near us, and Mrs Weiss tut-tutted about cinema stars, pop stars, and gratuitous publicity stunts. The roller-skaters unfurled a banner: COME BACK SOON, BUBBLES. WE LOVE YOU!

Through the crowd came a beaming figure in a cream rawhide jacket, snakeskin cowboy boots and a white stetson.

The figure stared straight at me and Mrs Weiss and smiled in this totally disarming fashion.

'Am I late?' he said in consternation, one ringed hand fluttering to his cheek.

Mrs Weiss saw the little yellow button.

'Mr LaSalle!' she gasped.

'*So* sorry,' he said, 'Boys, here we are: my bags, *s'il vous plaît*!'

The boys added an extravagant stack of cream and pink cases and bags to the mound. Mr LaSalle pulled out a lacy handkerchief.

'I can only say I'll miss you – *all* —' he declaimed to the entire throng. 'But it is a far, far better thing I do! When I come back to these uncivilised shores, I will be the most educated, cultured and fascinating person this side of the pond! Farewell!'

He kissed everybody, and I noticed that the Scarlett O'Hara lookalike by me had the faintest suggestion of a five-o'clock shadow. Goddam! Everybody in his retinue was a man! But men like I'd never seen or dreamed of. Men in frocks? Who the hell was this Mr LaSalle?

'You'd better go now – big boys don't cry,' he said, and they all drifted away, blowing kisses, waving and shouting at him: 'Write to us, darling! Give my love to the real Betty Windsor!'

'I shall go to the cafeteria,' said Mrs Weiss icily. 'You will wait for us here. And don't move.' She hurried away, her walk that of a woman who has had Too Much!

'Gracious heavens,' said Mr LaSalle, patting his hair, 'I loved the farewell committee, but the welcoming committee! My *dear*! Too, too, Baby Jane!'

'I was second last,' I said. 'Everybody went to the cafeteria.'

'It's so hard to leave!' he said, 'I only applied for this for fun – what are our fellow travellers like? And how rude of me! My name is Eugene LaSalle.'

'Monica Robinson. We have five preppies, two Southern Belles and a bunch of Dallas understudies.'

'Well, well, so we're the naughty children. But I do love Southern Belles – it's the voice, so Vivien Leigh, I declare. Sweet Jesus and all his blessed angels – is that *them*?'

Mrs Weiss was clicketty-clacking our way, with the Lady Constance Scholarships flocking behind her.

'I think we insist on seats together – smoking?' said Mr LaSalle, *sotto voce*.

'Yeah,' I said, relieved. The idea of spending five hours beside Rosamund, Melinda, Sam, Chuck, Wayne or John-boy did nothing for me. Who or whatever this Eugene LaSalle might be, his air of carnival and his gracious drawl appealed.

'We had better hurry to the departure lounge now that we are assembled,' said Mrs Weiss. Mr LaSalle winked at me and attached himself to her.

'What are the seating arrangements?' he asked ingenuously, 'I didn't realise Miss Robinson was on the Foundation. We're practically related! We'd like to sit together in a smoker, if it's possible.'

'We'll sort all that out at the desk,' said Mrs Weiss, 'You know each other? Of course.'

Smokers to the left, so we detached ourselves from the cluster of bright young America and found our seats. Mr LaSalle gave me the window, seeing as it was my first flight, and the clouds, darling, were quite *hallucinogenic*! Somehow he rustled a couple of drinks out of the sultry steward before take-off, and offered me a pack of pastel-coloured gold-tipped cigarettes. The steward leant over us, and I noticed eyeliner. Eyeliner? Also the musky scent my dear Mom always said was the sign of loose morals. The boy was a flagrant swaggering bawdy house, and I knew instinctively that none of it was for *my* benefit.

'Don't light *up* until we've really taken off and got high,' he said, raising one dark eyebrow and giggling. 'Regulations.'

'Thank you,' said Mr LaSalle to his departing back. 'Monica, my dear, I had to read an extraordinary play for this scholarship fiasco – the best line is "*Smoking's not the same without matches!*" They were all in an insane asylum, you see, and not allowed to play with fire. Now I know the truth of that statement!'

I was dying to smoke myself, and as soon as the stewards had mimed their way through life-jackets and radio facilities, Mr LaSalle slipped out an exquisite pearl lighter and put an end to our misery.

'So, which college of the great university are you assigned to?'

'Nordgarten,' I said.

'Praise the Lord! That's mine, too. We should keep each other sane. I was dreading having only a deadly earnest Yankee doodle dandy to spend my evenings with. What made you fling yourself on the bosom of Lady Constance Glynn?'

'It was my English teacher. She was really English, went to Nordgarten College, and it seemed like the best way of getting away from home for a couple of years. She gave me a lot of coaching and stuff. I'm more interested in England than English Literature.'

'I do know what you mean,' said Mr LaSalle. 'The night-life! I can't wait to find out exactly what heap of decadence the Pilgrim Fathers felt they had to leave. Do you know anyone in England?'

'Well, Margaret – the teacher – gave me some addresses. They're all professors. Could be interesting.' I wasn't entirely convinced.

'Well, I have a bunch of people to see – artistes, mainly.'

'Are you in the theatre – hell, what's your first name again?'

'Oh, forgive me!' he said, clicking his fingers at the sultry steward. 'Eugene. Momma named me for Eugene O'Neill, she must have known I'd take to the boards. But my stage name is Bubbles LaTouche, which I much prefer. I do a show – heavens! – *did* a show at Betty Windsor's, the drag bar in Baltimore.'

Drag bar? I didn't wish to appear ignorant.

'Was that your audience back at the airport?'

'My friends – my fans – you know,' he said. 'What are you drinking?'

'Bourbon usually,' I said.

'Would you care for champagne?' said Eugene. 'Nostalgia, you know. I named myself Bubbles the night that I first drank champagne. Do call me Bubbles, Monica, make me feel at home.'

I nodded. I knew what he meant about names. A shame I had only Noreen Jane Smith and Monica Robinson to choose from. And of course, I had once, briefly, been Sonya Dumbassova, the fool who'd admitted to being seventeen at just the wrong moment. Well, I'd never do that again. I liked this guy. He was polite enough to be interested in me, but was also honestly and totally fascinated and fascinating about himself.

'Be a darling and fetch us some champagne,' he said kittenishly to the steward, 'and a half-bottle of Jack Daniels, s'il vous plaît!'

'Mais, oui,' said the steward, with a wink.

Bubbles flapped an exquisite handkerchief around his face.

'Do I look florid?' he said anxiously. 'My heart races so for take-off. And I hate that wind-on-the-cheeks look – I'm a hothouse plant, a sort of ivory camellia, hardly a wild rose.'

'You look fine,' I said, amused at his vanity. It had never occurred to me that men bothered what they looked like. Well, Scoot would spend an age trying on shirts as if there was a world of difference between stripes and plaid. I thought it was because he was young. Bubbles excused himself – *must freshen up!* – and I sat back and looked out of the window.

We were above the clouds now. I'd seen this in movies a million times, and it was weird to actually be here, somewhere in mid-air, with only a few inches of steel and insulation fibre between me and free-falling. It was odd, too, to be sitting on an upholstered chair in the metallic tinkle of muzak, feet on a carpet like you were in a house: it was unreal. Real would have been flying like a bird, with the cold wind on my face, diving through the chill wetness of cloud, eyes narrowed against the dazzle of sunlight. Up here were clouds, up here it was never cloudy grey. Through breaks in the cloud I could see the lava flow of the waves, gun-metal grey with sombre navy tattered patches where the clouds threw moving shadows.

Bubbles sat back next to me, his blond curls combed to fluff, his face pale and smooth with powder.

'Believe me, it's the only way to travel,' he drawled, mixing Jack Daniels and champagne. 'Eight miles high and mildly intoxicated. Cheers! May England bring us both our hearts' desire!'

It was a helluva drink. I sensed that he needed a cue.

'And what's your heart's desire, Bubbles?'

'Well,' he said, smiling with what he meant as modesty, hands fluttering with studied ingenuity, 'I have to be honest and say, *entre nous*, that I hope to expand my horizons. Of course there's always the Big Romance. Some day my prince will come – you know? But, as Tennessee Williams said, when you love something more than making love, that's your life's work.'

That sounded sad to me. Sounded like making the best of a bad situation. Just like I'd had to when Margaret had put me and erotic love and perversion into the same sentence. I could still hear the stepped-on-a-slug revulsion in her voice. Maybe in England I'd get so used to English accents that I wouldn't turn and stare with a pain in my gut and my heart thundering. I longed for the day she'd be out of my thoughts and I wouldn't care.

'You see, I've found my life's work,' said Bubbles. 'Frankly, I'd rather be swishing around on stage than biting my nails by a silent telephone.'

It was way too close to home and I switched off while he chatted on beside me. Besides, what on earth could I love more than making love? Even my one-night stand with Pete had left me with delirious memories – and he was the wrong sex, the wrong person. Love was a word we'd only ever used about getting high on smoke or wild music. That night had been about need – oh, bullshit yourself some more, Monica, I thought, that night had been about knowing that Margaret wouldn't ever love me the way I loved her. Jesus! I was barely eighteen and I'd had and lost the love of my life. I drank to stop myself weeping.

'The magic of the footlights! The adulation of the crowd: it's my drug!' Bubbles broke into my thoughts.

I smiled and nodded so he'd go on.

'But what about you, Monica? Do stop me, I am the world's greatest egomaniac after the unfortunate Miss Streep. Secret for a secret: tell auntie your heart's desire.'

Her name is Margaret Courtland.

'As you say, the Big Romance,' I said, rolling a cigarette – how *Bogart*! murmured Bubbles – 'But I'm looking for someone else too. I was adopted. My mother's English.'

'Fascinating!' said Bubbles, all breathless débutante and yoo-hooing the sultry steward our way.

And that was true. I wanted to find someone who looked like me, who was maybe a bit like me. I felt a rush of warmth towards Mom, way back in What Cheer with only Pop and Scoot to scold and fret over. England was my new world now: at least I'd got that much from knowing Margaret the lion lady. And no one could say I hadn't done everything I knew how to be true to my love. Hell, if the plane crashed, would I regret one word, deed or moment? Joanne Lee Hunter, Tess, Pete, Maureen? *Je ne regrette rien!* I just wanted more of whatever my life was about.

Bubbles drew a silver swizzle stick from his bag and mixed another drink.

'Here's *to*?' he asked me.

'Here's to it all,' I said.

Suddenly I felt absurdly happy.